I0731797

I CHOOSE YOU

A SECRET BILLIONAIRE ROMANCE

KRISTA LAKES

ZIRCONIA PUBLISHING, INC.

ABOUT THIS BOOK

Step 1: Go to college. *Check.*
    Step 2: Find a job. *No luck.*
    Step 3: Start a family. *Whoa, one thing at a time.*

Alicia Chambers was stuck on Step 2. No matter how many resumes she sent out, she couldn't find a job in her dream field: phone app development. It seemed like most successful apps were started by a single inspired person in their basement, including the most recent craze, *Monster Go.*

If only Alicia could find her own inspiration for an app...

Drawn into the game *(research, she told herself)*, she meets a mysterious stranger who also plays. He's perfect for her: rich, handsome, and nerdy. However, despite formerly being in app development himself, Jacob seems to have left it all behind.

Between romantic dates and catching monsters in the game, Alicia finds herself growing closer to the mysterious man.

But it turns out he has more to do with this game than he told her. When she learns something that he deliberately kept hidden, will she flee his secretive life?

Will she let him know her own secret- that she's carrying a little gift from all their time "playing" together?

~

We sipped our wine and Jacob moved his hand gently up and down my lower back. I looked toward him, admiring the way the sunlight blanketed his face. He smiled when he caught me looking.

"You're cute," I said.

He leaned in and kissed my cheek. "No, you're the one who's cute."

I caught his face in my hands, and then angled in to kiss him. I had meant it to be a fairly quick kiss, something playful yet more than a peck on the check. But, when he kissed me, it quickly turned into something else.

Heat coursed down my spine, sending tingles of desire through my nerves. Jacob felt it too. He kissed me harder, pulling me into him with his hands and his mouth. I went from simply wanting a kiss to wanting so, so much more.

Panting, I sat back and pulled my hair from my face. I didn't want to be too forward, especially not since the other day where he had turned me down. If he wanted to keep going slow, I could do slow. It was respectful and honorable.

I liked that, but I was ready for a little speed. *Respectful* and *honorable* were overrated.

Moving slowly, I brought my hand to his arm and crawled into his lap so that I was straddling him.

I pressed my chest out a little, wanting him to notice.

When I did, his eyes moved down my front and then back to my face. His pupils dilated slightly, despite the fact that they were almost in direct sunlight.

He brought his mouth to mine, filling me with the taste of his lips. There was passion behind the kiss that made me heating. There was no way I was going to be able to back off again if he kept this up. I wanted him.

In between my legs and underneath the front of Jacob's slacks, I felt something that hadn't been there when I had first straddled him. His cock was already firm and pressing against me. I could feel it through my jeans. It was the sexiest thing to know that he wanted me as bad as I wanted him.

I kissed him again, and this time I found myself grinding down on the bulge. Jacob let out a guttural moan as I guided my body upward along his length. When I broke the kiss, I notice that the expression on his face had changed. He looked at me with wild eyes and licked his lips. No words needed to be exchanged. We both knew what we were feeling. It was an unspoken thing. We wanted each other and clearly we were going to take what we wanted. We were done waiting.

Jacob's hands drifted down my thighs and landed on my rear. He pulled me upward, sliding me along his length once again. My body tingled with delight and heat started to surge .

"Upstairs?" he asked.

I nodded, unable to speak coherently…

Don't forget to join my mailing list as well for updates! (clickable link)

This book is dedicated to Beth, Ana, Aimee, Anita, and Adrienne. Thank you for being my emergency readers! I couldn't have made this book without you!

I CHOOSE YOU

CHAPTER 1

This is going to hurt, I thought as I hurtled through space.

I wasn't quite sure what had caught the toe of my shoe, but somehow the floor was quickly coming up to greet me. It would be less than a second before my entire body slammed into the floor of the restaurant entryway, which was conveniently made of very hard-looking tile.

Just don't break anything, I prayed, holding my hands out, hoping that my arms would be strong enough to break my fall. It was going to be ugly and there was nothing I could do about it. I was inches away from colliding, when a pair of strong arms caught me around my waist and pulled me back up into a standing position.

"Careful," a man's voice said. The voice was calm and his hands were strong.

I was still wincing in anticipated pain as the stranger held me. I had been expecting to hit the floor, so it took me a second to realize that I had just been saved. His hands were on the top of my waist, holding me steady with a firm and safe grip.

"You okay?" he asked, not yet releasing me.

"I think I'm fine," I said, my voice shaking slightly. "You saved me."

"I just happened to be standing here when I saw you taking a dive," he said, making sure I was steady before letting me go. "It was all luck."

"Thank you," I muttered, feeling my face turn hot from embarrassment. I looked over at him to see he was gorgeous. He was tall with dark hair and an amazing smile. Even his glasses looked sexy. I looked down at the floor, suddenly shy.

Of course it would be a gorgeous guy who would catch me when I was about to face-plant. That was just how the world worked. I could feel the blush starting to burn I was turning so red. "That was a little awkward. It's these darn heels."

The man chuckled and shrugged. "Glad I was here to help. You have a nice day."

"Yeah, thanks," I said, trying my best to smile and not make eye contact. Luckily, he turned and walked away before I had to say anything else. I rubbed my arms, suddenly missing being held. It was a strange sensation, especially since the guy was a stranger. The feeling faded quickly as I took a deep breath. I smoothed my shirt and hurried to catch up to the rest of my family who were already at the hostess stand getting checked in.

"How many today?" the young girl asked as I arrived.

"Five, please," my mom answered after doing a quick head count.

"Follow me," the hostess said, grabbing some menus and walking us across the restaurant.

"That was a close one," my little brother Tommy said,

coming up behind me. "You almost had a pretty nasty fall back there."

"No joke, Tommy." I gave his small shoulder a gentle push. At thirteen years old he was still shorter than me, but I knew it wouldn't be for long. "How come a stranger had to save me? You were right behind me. You could have tried to help."

"I don't think I could have helped you in time," he said with a shrug. "I didn't even see you trip. Plus, that guy was there to save the day anyway, so it worked out. I can't believe how fast he grabbed you. Maybe he's a superhero in his spare time."

"You think there's a super hero in our middle of nowhere town?" I asked. "What would he be doing? Rescuing stray cows?"

"Clark Kent grew up in a small town. Maybe he's just here to relax." Tommy grinned at me. "And you know, cows are very grateful when you rescue them."

"Are you calling me a cow?" I asked, raising my eyebrows and and crossing my arms. Even though we were nine years apart, our sibling rivalry was still strong.

Tommy shot me a cheesy grin. "Not with Mom within earshot."

I rolled my eyes and kept walking after the hostess toward our table.

The rest of our group, which included my parents and best friend Caroline, were already at a booth on the far end of the restaurant. It took us a moment to get our seats and get comfortable.

"So, you girls are all graduated and done with college," my mom remarked, setting down her menu and gazing at Caroline and me fondly. "I'm so proud of you both. You two are *real* adults now, huh?"

"Ugh, I guess so." Caroline sighed. "I'm not sure how I feel about that."

"Yup, it's only downhill from here," my father said, adjusting his glasses. "You should start picking out your burial plots now. It's the only thing you have to look forward to."

"Charles!" my mother scolded in a joking manner. The rest of us around the table laughed.

"Oh, they'll find out sooner or later," he continued. "The best years of your lives are behind you. Now you have to get a job and pay bills. You guys are picking up dinner, right? That's what being an adult's all about."

He winked at us both. Dad and Mom had been the ones to invite Caroline and I out to celebrate being home and graduated from college. He had already said he was paying several times and for us to get anything we wanted.

"If only getting a job was easy as paying a bill," Carolina muttered, and I coughed a sympathetic laugh in agreement.

"Yeah, I think Alicia would agree with you on that one," my mother said and I looked up to meet her eyes. I had been home for a day and a half and the topic of employment had already been raised by my father. Several times.

My father was the first to pry about my post-college plans, and he didn't need to wait for graduation as an invitation. He had been on me since last summer, just before the beginning of my senior year. I knew he was just trying to make sure I could take care of myself, but it was a bit much.

I told him what I always did, that my plan was to apply for an internship at ZephTech to work on developing computer apps. He wasn't much of a fan of that plan because it required a hyper-competitive application and intern process, and that was far too much uncertainty for a man who never allowed his gas tank to get less than half full.

"You'll both find your paths," my mother assured us. "And in twenty years, you'll look back and laugh at the process."

"In twenty years, I'll be a high school English teacher still paying off loans and actively plotting ways to burn the school down," Caroline replied with a grin. "I can't wait."

"And I'll be somewhere in a cubical waiting for your smoke signal so I can do the same thing," I replied. We both laughed.

"Well, as long as you don't get caught." My mother shrugged. "I will be too busy traveling the world on your inheritance money to bail either of you out."

"It's up to you then, Tommy," I said, turning to my little brother. "You'll have to come break Caroline and me out of jail. I hope you're up to the task."

"I think I could plan a jailbreak," Tommy said thoughtfully. "I could at least bake you file in a cake or something."

"I've eaten the things you bake," I replied. "I think I'd rather be in jail."

"First of all, you wouldn't be eating it. You'd be getting the file out," Tommy explained. "And secondly, I'll be able to bake better in twenty years. Duh."

It was then that the waitress arrived with our drinks and took our food orders.

My father raised his glass of recently delivered tap beer. "To the start of new beginnings," he said as cheers.

"*To new beginnings*," everyone echoed. I sipped at my pale ale and tried not to worry about what exactly my new beginning was going to be.

"Hey, let me have a sip," Tommy whispered as I lowered my glass. I handed him my beer and he sipped slyly before passing it back. It made me wonder when the time would come where we would *actually* share drinks. It wasn't really that far away, I realized while subtly studying my brother. Time had a way of flying past without us realizing it.

"So Caroline, any idea on where you want to teach at?" Mom asked, restarting the conversation.

"Anywhere that needs a new English teacher," she replied, tucking a strand of shiny black hair behind her ear. "Right now, I've got to find somewhere that'll take on a first year teacher, which is trickier than it sounds."

"How's that going?" my father asked.

"Not so well," she said with a shrug. "I've had to expand my searches and apply for non-preferred grades. I just haven't gotten anything yet."

"I'm glad to hear you're working on it," Dad told her. He adjusted his glasses and looked over at me with raised eyebrows. I thought about throwing my beer at him, since I really was trying to find a job, but instead just smiled and took a sip.

"I'm sure Tommy would take you over his English teacher," my mother said, pulling my father's focus away from me. "We haven't been very pleased with her."

"I applied at the school, but I haven't heard anything back," Caroline replied. "Maybe you'll get lucky Tommy and get me next year instead."

I was glad that Caroline had joined us for our dinner. It was supposed to be a miniature celebration for our graduation, and it wouldn't have felt right without her. She was an honorary member of the family and had joined us for dinners for as long as I could remember, back when dinners were usually followed by a sleepover.

Caroline's company was also a great excuse to talk about someone else's unemployment instead of my own. It was almost a toss-up as to which one of us would find work first. At least with her here, my dad wouldn't use the entire meal to find out how many resumes I had sent out.

I tried to pay attention to the discussion about how terrible Tommy's teacher was, but the table next to us stood and left, giving me a clear view of the room. Instead of the conversation, I was drawn to something else. Or rather, someone else. It was the guy who had saved me from falling in the entryway.

From where I sat, I had a perfect view of his face. My first impression of him was dead on. Gorgeous. He was strikingly handsome, with dark hair combed to one side and a square jaw covered in beard stubble. He wore square dark framed glasses that instantly gave him the impression of intelligence. My stomach fluttered with the thought that I had been wrapped up in his arms not that long ago. Warmth filled my belly and my heart skipped a beat. He must have felt me looking at him, because he glanced up and smiled at me.

I nearly melted at the subtle flirtation and even more so when I noticed his eyes. They were sky blue, unlike any I had ever seen in real life. They were beautiful and intriguing. I smiled back to the man, willing myself not to blush. He nodded and then brought his gaze to his menu once again.

If my family wasn't here, I'd go over and ask him out, I thought to myself. And then shook my head. Even if my family wasn't here and I'd been alone, I still wouldn't have had the guts to go over and talk to him. Besides, what would I say? *Thanks again for saving me, maybe you could catch me again sometime?* It sounded horrible even inside my head.

The stranger across the restaurant set his menu down and then brought his attention to his cell phone. I couldn't stop watching him. He stuck out like a sore thumb in the family style restaurant. He was well-dressed and his mannerisms were smooth and masculine. It didn't feel like he belonged in a little town like ours, though I certainly wasn't complaining.

My attention was forced back to my table when the waitress walked up and placed a plate of food in front of me. The warm smell of seasoned chicken wafted up into my face like a transparent fog. My mouth watered in anticipation, temporarily distracting me from the beautiful stranger at the nearby table.

In school with Caroline, we only ever cooked different types of pasta for the most part. It was cheap and hard to mess up, and neither of us were particularly good cooks. I had become especially fond of Japanese noodles with tofu, because it was cheaper than chicken. As we inched closer to graduation the effort allotted to grocery shopping took more and more of a hit. Finally, we had stopped shopping altogether and our goal became simply to finish everything in the pantry. I was more than eager for a nice meal that wasn't cobbled together spaghetti noodles and peanut butter.

"This looks so good. Thanks for dinner, Dad," I said, flashing my dad a smile. I couldn't wait to devour a herb encrusted chicken breast.

"You're very welcome," Dad replied. He grinned and took a bite of his own meal. "How's yours, Tommy?"

"It's great," Tommy replied absently. He stared at his phone and pushed out his chair, already heading for the door. "I gotta go, but I"ll be right back."

"Tommy where are you going?" my mother called after him.

"Your food just came, buddy. Come on, sit down," my father said.

"I'll be right back," he shouted back. "Promise!" He was off before another objection could be spoken.

I watched him and then looked to my mother. "What was that about?" I asked.

"Just some phone game," she said. She shook her head like I had asked a rhetorical question. "He's been doing that all week. I've given up trying to stop him."

Caroline laughed. "He's a funny kid."

"Yes, he is," my mother replied with emphasis. "Never a dull day with that one."

"I bet you forgot what it was like having a little minion always chasing you around," my father said, taking another bite of food.

"No, I actually missed him a lot," I said. "And honestly he has matured a lot since I left, it's kind of crazy."

"He missed you, too," Mom assured me. "I wasn't the one who insisted on sending you all those cookie care packages."

"And lord knows we appreciated them," I told her. "I'm pretty sure that Caroline and I ate nothing but cookies for several meals."

"If I had known that, I would have sent you food!" my mother replied, looking shocked.

"It's what you do in college," my dad assured her. "Builds character."

"Or diabetes," Caroline whispered to me and I had to hold in a laugh.

Tommy returned to the table and slumped into his seat as only a pre-teenage boy could. He stared at his phone for another minute before putting it back in his pocket.

"Oh, welcome back," I said. "Thanks for joining us."

He looked at me and made a face that looked like it should have been accompanied with a stuck out tongue.

"The waitress is coming back to get your food," my father told him. "We told her you didn't want it."

Tommy rolled his eyes, knowing that our father was just messing with him as he dug into his cheeseburger and fries. "Thanks, Dad."

"Did you go outside?" I asked, taking a bite of my chicken. I looked past him to the windows and saw the twilight softly creeping in over the sidewalk, almost expecting to see some sort of tempting attraction instead of the city street.

"Yeah," he replied with a shrug, as if my question was a mere waste of time.

"And?" I prompted.

"And what?" He took another bite of his burger and shrugged.

"Nothing I guess," I told him. My mother just shrugged at me. Apparently this was usual for him.

"Have you sent in your application to ZephTech yet?" Caroline asked between bites of her fettuccine alfredo. I looked up at my father and wasn't surprised to find him looking over his glasses at me, waiting for me to answer.

"Almost," I told her. "I'm almost done. This application is more work than applying to grad school."

"What all do you have left?" Caroline asked. "I think last I heard you were working on some essay."

"I finished the *written questionnaire*," I said, stressing the term so as not to sound like a high school senior. "I have all the testing done and I met with their recruitment person for an interview before school ended, so that's done. Now, I just have to submit my resume with a cover letter."

"Submit or finish?" my father asked bluntly.

"Submit," I informed him, feeling a little defensive.

"That's intense," Caroline said. "Makes my applications seem easier."

"Well, it's a pretty competitive internship," I said, speaking more to the table than to Caroline alone. "Like, incredibly competitive. They only accept ten applicants out of the hundreds that they get."

"I know you'll get it," Caroline said and nudged me with her elbow. "I'd hire you in a heartbeat."

"Actually, I was hoping you could read over my cover letter before I submit it, if you don't mind," I said. Caroline did have her degree in English after all.

"Oh, absolutely," said Caroline. "Email it to me."

"Thanks, Caroline." I smiled at her. "I appreciate it. I really want this."

"What happens if you get the job?" Caroline asked. She pushed her empty plate away from her.

"If I do get accepted to their internship program, I'll work with the other nine interns designing software platforms for new apps. And we're all evaluated the whole time. Then, after six-weeks, they make *one* offer for a full-time position." I couldn't help but glance at my father who ate as he watched me speak. His face remained motionless.

"I know you've told me this before, but what's so special about ZephTech? Isn't there a company out there that would be easier to work for?" Mom asked.

"ZephTech designs games," I explained. "They've been my dream job since I was ten. They are the best of the best. Just getting the internship gets you in the door for almost every other job out there."

I looked at my plate of chicken and realized that I hadn't eaten much since the conversation began. Consciously, I forked a sizable bite to my mouth, hoping that someone else would take over the talking.

"We're crossing our fingers for you," my mother said. I was surprised both by the warm smile on her face and the way she'd sounded almost nostalgic. "You're going to do so many amazing things. You always do."

"What games do they make?" Tommy asked, finally joining the conversation.

"Nerd games," I replied, trying to be humorous.

"Seriously, what games?" Tommy pressed. "Do they have anything to do with Monster GO?"

"Monster GO? I don't thinks so," I answered. "But I'll show you their games when we get home."

Tommy looked far less excited than I expected.

"Do they make an app that'll get me a job?" Caroline said, her words backed by a faint sarcasm.

"You turn my cover letter into something genius, and I'll make the app for you," I said and Caroline smiled back at me.

"That's a deal," she said.

As my family continued their conversation, I looked back toward the table where the handsome man had been seated. Sadly, he was no longer there.

Bummer, I thought. *I would have liked to see him again.*

CHAPTER 2

> *Dear Alicia,*
>
> *We regret to inform you that the position you applied for as software engineer has been filled by a more qualified applicant. We wish you the best in your journey and hope you reapply next year.*

With an agitated sigh, I clicked the "delete" button on the email and put it in the trash along with all the others. It was the third email I had gotten that day and they all said the same thing, that my newly received college degree was worth practically nothing in the work force.

I spun my chair around away from the desk. At the same time, Tommy popped in through the door, unannounced.

"Why do you look so upset?" he asked, as he pushed his shaggy hair out of his eyes.

"Because I have a little brother who doesn't know how to knock," I replied, with a sarcastic smirk.

Completely ignoring me, Tommy strolled in and took a seat on my bed.

"Seriously, Alicia, you've been in here all day," he said. "You've been home from college for more than a week and I haven't seen you at all."

"I'm just really trying to find a job and I'm not having any luck," I said, shaking my head. "It seems like all I get are denial letters."

"What about that Zephtech job that you were talking about?" he asked. "I thought you had already started the steps to getting hired there."

"I *have* started, but there are like twenty steps to their hiring process. I'm on step five, and I haven't heard back from them in two days." I sighed loudly. "I worked really hard at my resume and cover letter for them. I even had Caroline look over it for me, but I have a feeling that I'm going to get an email from them soon that's just like all the others."

Tommy didn't really understand the full gravity of my situation. He had just turned thirteen, his world was still small, and his only real concern was how he'd spend his free days during summer vacation. I wished that I could still be that young and carefree. But alas, I was a college graduate and needed to start building my own life. It was time to grow up.

"Look, sis, you need to get out of the house," he said, standing up from my bed and walking toward me. "I've been playing this game on my phone and it's pretty fun. You should try it with me."

"A game?" I asked. "You mean the game you were playing at the restaurant the other day? Tommy, I don't have time for this."

"Why not?"

"I just told you that I need to be looking for work," I said, with a defeated sigh.

"Are you sure that's all it is?" he asked, with a snarky tone. "Or do you have to call your boyfriend?"

I shot him a dirty look. "I don't have a boyfriend, Tommy. You know that."

"Then get out of the chair and come play this game with me," he said, grabbing my hand and jerking me to a standing position. "It'll be fun."

"Fine," I said. "I'll go out with you for a half an hour but then I need to get back here."

"Deal," he said, leading me downstairs.

We got our dog Athena, leashed up and ready to go with us, then stepped out into the fresh summer air. We made our way straight toward the park in the center of town. As we walked, Tommy explained the game to me.

"It's called MonsterGo," he said, pulling out his cell phone. "You open up the app and then monsters pop up on your screen. They can show up anywhere, so you have to run all over town to find them."

Tommy snatched my phone out of my hand and quickly downloaded the game for me.

"There, now you can play too," he said.

I shrugged, seeing the game as the perfect opportunity to distract myself from the misery that was job hunting. We ran around the park for a bit and it wasn't long before I caught my first monster. It was called a "Stingly."

"This is actually kind of fun," I finally admitted.

"Told you," Tommy said. "Now come on, I want to show you a Monster Gym. It's where we can take the monsters we catch and have them fight other people's monsters."

"Tommy, I don't have all day," I said, crossing my arms.

"It's really close," he said. "Trust me. I'll have you back home soon, but I want you to see this. It's probably my favorite part of the game."

"Okay, but you have ten minutes and then we have to head back." As soon as the words came out, I realized that I sounded a bit like my mother.

Luckily, Tommy wasn't lying when he said this so-called "Monster Gym" was only a block or so away. And when we got to the church on the corner, a huge group of people was standing out in front.

"What's going on here?" I asked, glancing around at all the people. It seemed like most of the town was there.

"Team Red is getting attacked by Team Blue," Tommy explained, pulling out his phone and starting to press buttons furiously.

I sighed. "Tommy, I have no clue what you're talking about."

"This location is a Monster Gym." He rolled his eyes as if what he just said made all the sense in the world.

"Looks like a church to me," I said, trying to walk away.

"It *is* a church, but it's also a Monster Gym. It's part of how this game works. It combines the real world with the digital world. Right now, my team is controlling the Gym," Tommy explained. He stood in my path so I couldn't leave. "Team Blue is trying to take it over, so I'm sending in one of my monsters to defend against the attack."

"Sounds pretty serious," I said, sarcastically. I played around on my phone, but there weren't any monsters around currently and I wasn't rated high enough to enter the gym yet.

I looked around, watching everyone play on their phones. At first, I thought it was kind of dumb that everyone was just standing there, but the longer I watched, the more I saw people interacting and being friendly. For being an individually played game, people were being remarkably social.

"No, no, NO, NO!" Tommy suddenly cried, mashing on

his phone screen. He looked about ready to throw it on the sidewalk. "This can't be happening!"

"What's wrong, Tommy?" I asked. "Are you losing?"

"My phone locked up right in the middle of my battle." He frowned and looked like someone had kicked his dog. "I'm letting my team down."

"It'll be okay," I promised. "Just restart. I'm sure everyone will understand."

"I did restart," Tommy told me. "The game is totally locked up for me. We're going to lose the gym and it's going to be my fault!"

"Team Red?" a man asked, coming up beside Tommy.

"Yep," Tommy responded, not even looking up. But I stopped and stared. It was the same man who had caught me at the restaurant the other day. He was still beyond gorgeous. Instead of the glasses, he wore sunglasses, but they still looked like prescription glasses.

"Me too," the man said to Tommy, pulling out his phone. "You said your game locked up?"

Tommy nodded glumly. "I'm stuck on the loading screen."

"Did you log out? Sometimes that reloads your user data and will get you back in the game," the man told him.

Athena came up to him and sniffed his hand. The man quickly pet her on the head, and Athena leaned into it. If my dog thought this guy was okay, I guess I could let him talk to my little brother. He looked up briefly at me and smiled as Tommy continued to follow his instructions.

"I'm back in," Tommy announced, relief filling his features. "Now, to keep the gym under our control."

"Good to have you back in the battle." The man studied his phone screen. "Hmmm, a leveled up Stingly would take care of this situation in a heart beat."

"You're right," Tommy agreed, but he frowned. "But I don't have one."

"I do," I interrupted, holding up my phone.

I was just glad that I had a reason to join in the conversation with this guy. Up until thirty seconds ago, I had been sure I would never see him again. I hoped my Stingly would be enough to catch his attention.

Tommy chuckled. "No, you don't, Alicia. They're super rare."

"Yes, I do," I insisted. "Look for yourself. I caught it this morning."

Tommy snatched my phone and his eyes lit up, but just for a moment. "She *does* have one, but we can't use it. It's not strong enough yet."

"That's too bad," the guy said. He winked at me before turning back to Tommy. "Just send in your best monsters and I'll do the same. We can't let Blue take over this gym."

Tommy nodded in agreement and tapped away on his phone. The guy flashed me a quick smile before focusing on Tommy again. It was sweet how the two of them were interacting.

I watched as my hero made himself an instant friend with my little brother based purely on the game. They spoke as if they were soldiers about to go into battle and I found myself wishing I was further along in the game so that I could play along with them. They looked like they were having a blast.

I stood awkwardly nearby, wishing I could join in on the conversation, but knowing that I didn't stand a chance. I'd look like an idiot if I attempted to talk about the Monsters in this game that I knew nothing about. Instead, I just observed the two of them.

I wondered what he did for a living, and what kind of

job he had that would allow him to play a game in the park in the middle of the day. *Maybe he's unemployed, just like me.* I chuckled to myself. *Or maybe he somehow gets paid to be good-looking.*

The man pressed something on his phone before looking up at me and grinning.

"Hi. Sorry I just walked up on you guys like that," he said. His blue eyes were friendly and bright. "I just overheard you guys and knew you were playing the game. That's what I'm here for too."

"No problem." I swallowed and shrugged nonchalantly. "I'm just glad my brother got to play with someone that knows what they're doing."

"I'm Jacob," he said, holding out his hand.

"Alicia." I took his hand and gave a firm shake. I wished I had spent a little more time on my hair before leaving the house. That, and I was fairly sure that there was a hole in the sleeve of my t-shirt. I hoped he hadn't noticed, because I felt like there was a neon sign pointing to it now that he was standing next to me.

"Hi, Alicia." He smiled again as he let go of my hand. "I'm surprised your brother hasn't gotten you hooked on the game yet."

I laughed, shuffling my feet on the pavement. "I like it, I think. I just haven't played very much so I don't really know what to do."

"It's a pretty fun little game. You should give it a chance," he said. He was smiling again, and I couldn't help but smile back. His easy grin was infectious.

"Maybe I will," I replied. "Thank you again for catching me the other night."

"It was my pleasure," he assured me. "I would be happy to catch you any time."

I blushed slightly. "I bet you say that to all the girls you save."

He leaned forward to whisper. "Just the pretty ones."

This guy was all confidence and charm. I found it rather appealing. There was nothing fake to it, nothing that said he was simply playing a part. This was just his natural charm. I could appreciate the compliment.

"Still, thank you again for saving me," I said.

He waved his hand through the air. "It really was no trouble. I'm just glad you didn't actually fall and break your wrists. Then you wouldn't be able to play the game."

I laughed. "I get the feeling you want me to play more."

"Only if you want to," he said. "But I promise that you'll get hooked at some point if you do. It only gets better the more you play."

"Is that so?" I tucked a strand of hair behind my ear and bit my lip before I could stop myself.

"Look, it sounds like you're pretty hesitant," he said, rubbing at the stubble on his chin. "But if you wanted to learn more, maybe we could hang out and play some time?"

Is he asking me out? I wondered. I hoped so. He was cute and I was enjoying this. Talking with him was easy and comfortable, even if we were talking about a game. It would definitely be the first time a phone app had netted me a date.

"A Monster date?" I joked.

"I was just thinking that we could at least get you to level five," he offered. There was that smile again. He had to know the effect it had on women. "That way you can help your brother defend this gym."

"I'd love to play with you. I mean, play *the game* with you." I blushed, as I stumbled over my words. My stomach twisted into a happy, excited knot.

"Okay, well how about tomorrow then? Same time?" he asked. His smile somehow got bigger and even more friendly. My knees threatened to go all wobbly.

Tommy chimed in. "That works for me!" I had completely forgotten that he was there.

I shot my little brother a nasty look, but he just grinned at me. I decided I could tell him on the way back home that there was no way in heck he was coming with me to meet Jacob the next day. If he came, the date really would be all about the game, and I wasn't really interested in playing that much.

"That sounds perfect," I said, ignoring Tommy. "Should we meet here?"

"Actually, no, let's meet over at the fountain. We can walk around the park and pick up a few monsters, and hopefully get you enough experience points so that you can level up," he explained. "We'll be battling for the gym together in no time."

This game suddenly seemed like the greatest invention of all time.

"Perfect," I said, the word coming out a little more breathless than I wanted. I didn't want to appear too eager.

We looked at each other for just a moment and I felt that tingling of excitement inside of me. Was this the beginning of something? I hoped this would lead to a real date.

Jacob's phone vibrated and he glanced down. He pressed on his screen before turning and high-fiving Tommy.

"Looks like our team was able to defend the gym," Jacob announced, putting the phone back in his pocket.

"I knew we could handle it," Tommy replied. "Good job."

"You too," Jacob said, ruffling Tommy's hair. "We took care of business today."

I watched their interaction and it warmed my heart.

Jacob didn't appear to see Tommy as some annoying little kid, but instead he was just another warrior in this game, just as ready and able as he was. It was nice to see and somehow made me even more excited about the little get together that was planned for the following day.

"Alright, you two, I've got to get back to my apartment," Jacob said. "I'm still unpacking after a long move and this was just my break."

"You just moved here?" I was excited. That meant he lived here. He wasn't just driving through or here for the weekend.

"Yes. Just a couple of days ago." He placed his hand on my upper arm, giving it a gentle squeeze. "But I'll see you tomorrow."

"Yeah, yeah, definitely," I said, nodding quickly. "Sounds great."

Jacob walked off and I watched him leave. My eyes were locked on him the entire time as he made his way to the street corner, before disappearing from view behind the massive church that stood nearby. I nearly forgot to breathe.

"Alicia, maybe you should take a picture of him. It'll last longer," Tommy said, as he grabbed my wrist and tugged on it. "Come on, let's go. The Monster Gym is no longer under attack by the blue team. We don't have to stay around here."

I felt frozen in place, mystified by the charming man who had just unexpectedly asked me out on a date. Or at least a semi-date.

"Come *on*," Tommy pleaded, still pulling on my wrist. "I have things to do."

"Okay, okay. First I can't get you to leave, and now I can't leave fast enough." I shook my head at him. "You're ridiculous."

Finally, I got my feet to move and I followed Tommy

back to the fountain. He took his place on the wall, just catching Monsters and laughing with some other kids his age who were also playing the game. I could have played with them, but didn't. I wanted to wait until tomorrow to play with Jacob. So, instead, I walked around, exploring the park and letting my mind wander.

My interaction with Jacob had given me a burst of energy. The burned-out feeling that I had experienced that morning in my bedroom had all but vanished and was replaced with a tingling excitement. There was something new on the horizon and even if it was just a silly meet up with a cute guy, it was infinitely better than applying for jobs I'd never get.

For the first time all week, I felt hopeful. There was something tangible to look forward to. Jacob had no idea the gift he had just given me.

I led Athena into the grass a little ways away from the fountain and we walked in a giant circle around a massive old oak tree. I was giggling to myself like a little girl with an uncontrollable goofy smile plastered across my face. I'm certain if someone had seen me, they'd have thought I'd lost my mind. But what did I care? My self-esteem was through the roof. A cute guy came out of nowhere and asked me out. After the constant rejection in the job market, I was suddenly worthwhile again. I felt beautiful, even with my tangled hair and threadbare t-shirt. It didn't matter. I had a date.

CHAPTER 3

*T*he sun shone brightly and birds chirped as I walked Athena towards the park. I had made sure I looked good today, so my confidence was high. I could do this. It wasn't really a date. It was just meeting a cute guy.

A *really* cute guy.

My initial confidence faded as I stepped onto the path that led into the park. First dates, even if they weren't really dates, were not my forte. I always managed to say something far too nerdy. I liked computers and science, and I had more than one date never call me back because I started talking about programming or computer languages better than they did.

I ran my fingers through my hair and then over my summer dress, making sure that everything was in order. It was too late to make a different first impression with Jacob, but I figured I could polish up my third impression the best I could. My heart beat quickly, and I drew in a slow breath to calm myself down.

Nearing the fountain, I noticed that there were a handful of people standing around it, just like the day before. They were all looking at their phones and swiping their screens, obviously playing the game. My eyes scanned over the small crowd and landed on the man I was there to meet. He was seated on the edge of the fountain, with the water behind him. His elbows were on his knees and his fingers were interlocked. He was wearing a white button-down shirt with gray slacks and dark brown shoes. It was nerdy, but attractive nerdy. As soon as he noticed me, his face brightened with a smile.

Okay, Alicia. Don't act weird, just relax and have fun, I told myself as I approached him.

"Hi there," he said, standing up to give me a casual hug.

I wrapped my arms around him, and the intoxicating scent of his cologne entered my nose. It was clean and crisp and reminded me of summer evenings.

"How are you?" I asked, as I released him from the hug and took a step back.

"Fantastic," he replied. He pulled off his sunglasses and slipped one of the earpieces into the neck of his shirt. His light blue eyes locked with mine, causing my knees to go weak. There were depths to those eyes that I knew I could get lost in, if I let myself.

Athena leaned in and sniffed him, and this time seemed genuinely excited to see him.

"This is a pleasant surprise. I honestly wasn't sure if you were going to come meet me this morning." He ran a hand through his short hair and for a moment I wondered if he was as nervous as I was.

I cocked my head to the side and flashed a playful smile. "What do you mean?"

"You obviously aren't too into playing Monster GO." Jacob shrugged. "Yesterday, it seemed pretty clear that your brother is the one who really likes to play."

"You're right about that," I agreed slowly. I tucked a strand of hair behind my ear. "But maybe playing the game wasn't the only reason I wanted to show up today."

His smile grew wide. "Maybe playing the game wasn't the only reason I *invited* you."

A thrill went through me from scalp to pinkie toes. He liked me. And I was already head over heels for him, almost literally. He had caught me once before, but this time I was looking forward to the fall, especially if it was falling with him.

"How about we hang out and get you to level five while we get to know each other?" he asked, motioning to the park behind him. "Unless you'd rather not play Monster GO at all. We could just walk around the park."

"No, let's play. It sounds fun," I insisted. "Plus, if you teach me how to play then I can finally get Tommy off of my back about it."

Jacob chuckled. "I'm an only child, so I wouldn't know what it's like to have to deal with a younger sibling. But Tommy actually seems like a pretty cool kid. I've met some young ones that drive me nuts and he definitely wasn't one of them."

"You're just being nice because you two happen to be on the same team," I replied with a laugh.

"I'm not saying one way or the other. It's possible that's why I got along with him, though," he said, with a playful wink. "Now come on, let's get you leveled up."

We both pulled out our phones and opened up the app. Jacob quickly explained more of the game play, pointing to his phone and showing me how to get the most out of the game. It made so much more sense when he explained it and I could see more of the appeal of the game.

Together we walked slowly around the fountain, waiting

for a monster to show up so that we could catch it. Athena followed dutifully behind us, her blond shaggy tail wagging slowly as we went.

"What got you into playing?" I asked as we made our second circle around. "You seem to know a lot about it."

"Not really," he said with a shrug.

"You aren't secretly one of the developers or something?" I teased.

Jacob tripped on the sidewalk and managed to catch himself just in time.

"Are you okay?" I asked, putting my hand on his arm to make sure he was steady. I wasn't ready for the thrill that went through my body at touching him.

"I'm fine," he assured me. "Just tripped over my own feet. You know as well as I do how easy it is."

He gave me a wide smile. His cheeks were bright with color that I could only assume came from nearly falling. I looked back and couldn't see what he had tripped on, but I knew that it could have been anything.

"So, what are you doing in town?" he asked, changing the subject.

"Um..." I smiled nervously. I wanted to impress him, but my reason for being here wasn't exactly glamorous. I decided to just go for the truth. "I just graduated and I'm living with my parents while I look for a job."

"Here?" Jacob asked, looking around as if there were available jobs around the park.

"Anywhere, really." I shrugged, trying my best to stay nonchalant and positive. "I need the free rent while I look."

"I can understand that." Jacob nodded. "What's your degree in?"

"I studied software engineering, system analysis, stuff like that," I replied slowly. This was the part where I either lost or impressed guys. "But my actual degree is in computer programming."

"Seriously?" he asked, his eyes widening with surprise.

"Yeah, seriously." I laughed. "Why does everyone always sound so shocked when I say that?"

"I just don't meet a lot of pretty girls who like computers, I guess," he replied.

My face felt hot.

"What about you?" I asked. I wanted to change the subject to take the focus off of me, and my reddened face. "Tell me *your* story."

"I actually work in software development. Or, I guess, I *did*. Until I moved out here to get away from it all," he said.

"You're in software development?" I asked. "That's basically my dream job."

"It's a pretty good job," he said. "But it's definitely not what I expected. There's a lot of things that no one can tell you about until you're actually neck deep in the business."

"I guess that's true," I said. "Even so, though, I would kill for that job. Actually, I would kill for *any* job right now, but even more so for a decent position in something that I went to school for."

Jacob smiled apologetically as he looked me over. "Not able to find any work, I take it?"

"No, nothing I want to do. I've probably sent a hundred resumes and have had no response at all." I sighed as we rounded a corner. "If I don't get a reply soon, I'm going to have to scoop ice cream for the summer to make some money."

"Things will work out. I'm sure of it." He placed his hand onto my shoulder and gave it a reassuring squeeze. My dad had told me the same thing a thousand times, but for some reason, when Jacob said it, it seemed to truly resonate with me. It made me feel like things really *would* work out.

"I hope you're right," I said. "Because honestly, I don't want to scoop ice cream."

"I actually love ice cream." He grinned at me as he put his hand on his chest like he was admitting to something important.

"But do you want to scoop it for a living?" I asked.

"No, but I'd buy it from you," he replied with a grin. "You'd be the best tipped ice-cream scooper there."

Another blush heated my face and I looked down, pretending to focus on my phone.

"What kind of software did you develop?" I asked, sincerely wanting to know more about him.

He hesitated, as if forming his answer carefully. He also looked around at the other people around, as if they would overhear us. Of course, they were all buried in their phones, so he turned to me and answered.

"All kinds. I started out working for a company that custom designed human resources software for corporations. I couldn't stand working in that world, though. It felt like I was the face of the 'the man' and I cringed every time I stepped foot into that office." He crinkled his nose. "The work felt so empty and meaningless. I'd say it was simply uninspiring, but that word doesn't give it justice."

"What did you do?" I asked, genuinely interested.

"I started working for myself, building websites and apps. Just doing whatever it took to make ends meet. I even came up with a few of my own apps," he explained. "I can definitely say that things have worked out for the better. Leaving the corporate world and working for myself was one of the best decisions I ever made."

"That sounds amazing," I said with a small sigh. I was

rather impressed. "I wish I knew how to start my own business. That way I wouldn't even have to apply for a job. I could also take the day off whenever I wanted."

"That's true," he said. "Except as a business owner, you never really get a day off. The work always seems to draw you back in, no matter how hard you fight it."

"I don't know, it can't be that bad," I said smiling at him. "It means you get to show the unemployed how to play games."

He grinned at me as we started another lap around the fountain. I couldn't help but smile back. Not only was he handsome and charming, but it turned out that he was also driven. I glanced around, looking for cameras hidden in the trees.

Surely, this must be some kind of reality show that I'm on because this guy can't be real, I thought. Cute, sexy, charming, and apparently a successful business owner. Why couldn't I have met a guy like that in college?

"What is your company's name?" I asked. I would have to look it up. Maybe they were hiring. "Are you still running it now that you're living here?"

Before he could answer my question, our phones vibrated. We both glanced down at the same time to see the Monster GO app flashing on the screen.

"There's a Buugybuug nearby," he said. He put his hand on the small of my back to turn me in the right direction. "It's not a rare monster, but you should catch it anyway. Anything you can do to get experience points will help get you leveled up."

Talking with Jacob, I had forgotten we were playing a game. I lifted my phone, and so did at least five other strangers around us. With a swipe, I caught the little cartoon creature. The catch gave me a grand total of five monsters in my inventory.

"See, it's easy," Jacob said, holding up his phone. His inventory screen looked way fuller than mine did.

"I'm still shocked at how much of a worldwide craze it's started. It's insane." As much as I fought it at first, I was starting to see how this game could be fun.

He laughed. "You're telling me. I never would have expected this game to become the cultural phenomenon that it has."

"Maybe that's all I need to do," I said with a laugh. "If I can create an app like this, I'll become a millionaire and not have to work ever again."

"Sounds easy," he replied. "I expect you on the cover of Forbes any day now."

Our conversation was interrupted when a group of younger kids nearby screamed out in excitement. The noise was quickly followed by the familiar tune of the local ice cream truck. It turned the corner and pulled onto the frontage road that ran alongside the edge of the park. The kids all scurried away, running frantically toward the utility truck carrying their favorite treats.

"You know, I wouldn't normally want something like ice cream at ten in the morning," he said, tipping his head toward the screaming. "But sometimes a craving hits and you just *have* to get an orange creamsicle."

"I *love* orange creamsicles," I said, grinning like a kid. "Especially for breakfast."

"It's settled then." Jacob grabbed my hand and we walked quickly toward the ice cream truck.

My heart skipped a beat as our fingers intertwined. I wasn't expecting to be holding hands with him so quickly, but I liked it. I didn't want to pull away. His touch felt right.

We joined the back of the line, holding hands the entire time until we finally got to the window to place our order. I actually hated letting go of his hand, even though I was rewarded with a delicious sugary treat. He ordered three of the orange treats and paid with cash.

"I haven't had one of these since I was a kid," I said, carefully opening the plastic wrapper as we walked away.

"I have to be honest..." Jacob replied, taking a big bite out of his. "I actually get one every time I see an ice cream truck. I would have screamed out like those kids did, but I didn't think that would make a very good impression."

I laughed. "I wouldn't have judged you. Everybody has their quirks and maybe yours is ice cream in the morning. Do you also need two of them for yourself?"

He shook his head. "One's for Athena." Before I could object, he held the ice cream out. Athena took two big bites before I squealed, "Stop!" and pushed away the ice cream. Jacob dropped it and Athena licked it up off the ground, obviously not stopping for anything. I thought it was adorable.

We strolled back to the fountain side by side. I kept hoping he'd reach for my hand again. The song from the ice cream truck faded into the distance as it pulled away, looking for the next group of sweet-tooths to profit off of. We took a seat on a wooden bench near the fountain and Athena sat on my feet, leaning into me.

"Do you really like playing Monster GO?" Jacob asked after a moment. "You said you can see the appeal, but I'm wondering if you actually enjoy it. If you're not having fun playing it, then we don't have to. There's obviously no pressure to play."

"I like it well enough. I think if I had designed the app,

then I'd probably have done a couple of things different." I shrugged and took another bite of my morning dessert.

He lifted his eyebrows and faced me. "Really? Like what?"

I shrugged. "I don't know. It would be nice for the streets to have their names on them, like a real map. It would also be nice to have a searchable map, you know so that you could see if something were going on at your destination or even plan a trip based on what you can find on the map."

Jacob nodded in agreement. "I *heard* that the developers looked into it, but decided it would be too much of a drain on people's limited data plans."

"It could if you did it the traditional way," I told him. "But, if you just adjusted the interface a little, it wouldn't take much data at all. There's another app, it's actually for driving directions, that has something similar that would work perfectly."

"Sounds like they should look into it again." He smiled again. "It's a good idea. I hadn't even thought of looking at non-game apps for ideas."

"It's just the way my mind works," I replied. "I'm always analyzing things like this. Sometimes I do it to websites, or to computer programs. I try to think about what I'd change to make something better or more enjoyable. I know I'm making myself sound like a total nerd here. It's just something I do."

"I love it and totally understand," he confessed. "I'm a bit of a nerd myself."

"Without your glasses, you don't look like it." I teasingly narrowed my eyes and took another bite of my ice cream with a grin. It was cold and delicious.

"Neither do you," he replied with a smile. "You have some on your face."

He reached over, gently wiping a smudge of orange from my cheek. I wasn't even quite sure how it had gotten there, but his touch sent a chill through me and I felt my heart flip flop.

"Thanks," I said, my voice coming out breathless and girlish.

Jacob had his creamsicle in his right hand as he reached his left over my shoulder. His fingers dropped down, gently touching the top of my arm. I scooted a little closer to him, his magnetic eyes drawing me closer.

Everything stopped. The kids laughing in the background faded out, the birds quieted down. Even Athena's panting seemed to silence. All I could hear was my heartbeat, thudding inside of my chest. There was tension in the air, but it was the good kind of tension. The kind that made my hands and feet tingle with delight, adrenaline bursting into my veins.

He leaned in a little closer. I could feel his breath against my cheek. The smell of his cologne wafted off of his shirt. My eyes closed halfway as I anticipated Jacob making his move. He went in for a kiss, bringing his lips toward mine slowly and sensually. We almost touched. There was a centimeter at most between us. It was going to be amazing and incredible and the best kiss of my entire life.

"Hey, what are you guys doing?" a voice said from behind us.

I didn't even have to turn around to know who it was. I'd have recognized that annoying little voice anywhere.

Tommy, I thought.

"Are you guys going to kiss or something?" Tommy asked, stepping around to the front of the bench.

Jacob pulled away and cleared his throat. He shifted in his seat, trying to play it cool. It was the first time I'd seen him even a little bit flustered, but he shrugged and was suddenly totally collected yet again.

"No, we were just hanging out, playing some Monster GO," Jacob explained.

"Tommy, what in the *hell* are you doing here?" I asked, doing my best to stay calm.

"Last I checked, we live in a free country," he said, as he crossed his arms to stand his ground in front of me. "I finished cleaning my room and Mom said I should come find you. It was just lucky I looked here first."

"Tommy, I'm going to give you three seconds to turn around and go home." I stated, my words slow and measured. Inside, I was ready to pummel the kid for interrupting what would have been an amazing first kiss.

"Or *what*?" he snapped back. "What, Alicia? *What* are you going to do?"

"Three." I narrowed my eyes.

"Whatever, I'll just tell Mom if you try to hurt me." He took a small step back, but kept his chin up defiantly. "I told you I wanted to come play Monster GO."

"Two."

"I'm not moving," Tommy said, but he glanced around like he was planning his escape.

"One," the last word came out of my mouth and I took a step forward. Tommy's faux bravery faded instantly and he ran quickly away, screaming out at the top of his lungs. A few people in the park looked over. I had only taken one step forward, but it was enough to get my point across.

"You know, I don't mind if your little brother hangs out with us," Jacob said quietly. "It's not a big deal."

I sighed and sat back down on the bench. Tommy had run over to the oak tree nearby and was standing there with his tongue out at me.

"He wasn't supposed to come with me today," I said. "He promised that he'd stay home and leave me alone for a little while. He's a great kid, but I'm just not used to having someone too young to drive around all the time. It's different living with him than it is just coming home for a holiday."

"Let me go talk to him," Jacob offered. "I have a way with kids."

I turned to face him, flashing an expression that showed just how insane I thought he must be for offering something like that. When Tommy wanted something, he could be as stubborn as me. It was definitely a family trait. "You sure?"

Jacob just chuckled as he stood up from the bench. "I'm going to give it a try."

He turned and made his way toward Tommy. *This ought to be good,* I thought. I sat on the bench, petting Athena. I had no idea what Jacob was going to do to convince Tommy to leave him alone for a while.

The two were out of earshot, but in perfect view. Jacob strolled up and knelt down. I saw them exchange a few words. A few seconds later, Tommy smiled as he nodded quickly. They gave each other a high five and then immediately after, Tommy turned and skipped away, making his way back across the park in the direction of home.

What the...? I thought. *No way.*

Jacob came and sat back down on the bench with a relaxed smirk. The man was pure confidence with the ability to back it up.

"How did you just do that?" I asked in complete disbelief. "What kind of magic do you have?"

He just shrugged like it was nothing. "I told him that it was incredibly important that I spend the time with you to get you leveled up in the game."

"That's it?" I crossed my arms and narrowed my eyes. There was no way that was all he said.

"Pretty much." He shrugged and grinned at me.

I playfully slapped Jacob's shoulder. "I know for a fact that it took more than that to get him to go away. I know Tommy, and he's *not* easily persuaded. What else did you say?"

"You really want to know?" His blue eyes sparkled as he waited for me to answer. "It's my amazing secret ability."

"Yes, tell me," I begged. I needed to know how he had performed this miracle.

Jacob shrugged. "I gave him ten bucks."

"Seriously?" My jaw opened and stayed there.

"Yeah. Ten bucks for ten minutes alone with you," he admitted. He grinned sheepishly as he smoothly wrapped his arm over my shoulder once again. "It was worth every penny."

"I can't believe you did that," I said, laughing so hard I nearly fell off the bench. It was one of the funniest things I had ever heard, and also a pretty darn good way of getting Tommy to get out of our hair. "But I like the technique. It's also another reason why I need a job so I can make some money. Maybe I can start getting Tommy to listen to me with a little bit of cash..."

He didn't wait for me to stop talking, he just leaned in and brought his lips to mine. He took what he wanted, what he knew I wanted, without waiting another second.

I gasped, as the air was practically pulled out of my lungs in shock. Our lips were electric, sparking with energy as they touched. I closed my eyes and brought a hand to Jacob's cheek. For a moment, he and I were the only ones in the entire park. The entire world, for that matter.

The passion between us was so apparent. It felt like we

had known each other for decades, not days. This was more than just a basic first kiss. It was a first kiss that promised more kisses. It promised going beyond kissing. It was the kind of thing that made me feel more alive than I had in a long time.

After what seemed like a beautiful eternity, we slowly broke the kiss. But we only stayed apart long enough to grab a breath of air and glance into each other's eyes. Our lips collided once more. A moan crept up into my throat, so soft that it didn't make it to my mouth. My senses exploded as we opened our lips just enough to let the tip of our tongues touch, dancing passionately.

Our phones vibrated. I would have kissed him like that all day if I had had the chance. We slowly opened our eyes and pulled apart. The interruption was annoying, but since it had affected our moment anyway, we decided to see what the notification was all about.

"There's a Monster nearby," Jacob laughed. He casually glanced down at his phone before slipping it back into his pocket. "But who cares about that?"

He kissed me again. Our phones continued to vibrate, attempting to notify us of the Monster that was close. I didn't care, though. It was just a game, and what mattered in that moment was what was right in front of me.

My hands drifted from Jacob's cheeks, to his shoulders and around to his chest. My fingers landed on the top button of his shirt. I paused there, wishing I could undo just the top button and let myself in to feel some skin. I wanted to. I wanted nothing more than that. But I couldn't. We were in a public park, and I knew that Tommy was likely somewhere nearby, spying on us.

Thinking of my little brother reminded me that I had responsibilities. I couldn't just sit and make out in the park like some teenager. Even though it was fun. The morning was ending, and I needed to get home.

"Can I see you again?" I asked, pulling back slightly and watching his reaction. "This was fun."

"Absolutely," Jacob replied. His smile was warm and genuine. "I'll bring us some replacement creamsicles next time we hang out."

My eyes widened and I looked beside me to where I had dropped my frozen treat. During that passionate kiss, the orange Popsicle had become the last thing on my mind. It laid on the bench, melting in the hot sun. Jacob had dropped his as well, and it was now on the grass being enjoyed by Athena.

"Whoops." I bit my lip, feeling a little bit silly that I had let myself get so drawn into the kiss that I had forgotten about the outside world entirely.

"Totally worth it," Jacob said, with a grin. "Want to do it again tomorrow?"

My heart fluttered and I knew I had a dopey grin plastered all over my face. "Yes."

Jacob's face lit up. He had the most amazing smile I had ever seen.

"Tomorrow? Same time?" Jacob asked, hope filling his voice.

I did the mental math as quickly as possible. I could still apply for my jobs and do this. In fact, I would do just about anything to do this again. "Yes, that would be perfect."

Jacob grinned and he offered me his hand to stand up from the bench. I didn't want him to let go, but I knew I would need to go home eventually.

"Your ten minutes are up," Tommy announced, walking up boldly. "I can give you another ten if you want..."

Jacob chuckled. "I like your business sense, kid, but I should probably attempt to get some work done today."

"Your loss," Tommy informed him.

"Most definitely my loss." Jacob met my eyes. "I'll see you later, Alicia."

I grinned. "See you later, Jacob."

I couldn't wait.

CHAPTER 4

"*N*ow you're doing it, too, Alicia?"

My mom's voice caused me to look up from my phone. She set a plate in front of me. We were having T-bone steak, with corn and mashed potatoes for dinner.

"What did you say, Mom?" I asked, setting my phone to the side. "Sorry, I was distracted."

"You've been staring at your phone for the past ten minutes." Mom frowned at me "Are you playing that same thing that Tommy has been playing for the past couple of weeks?"

I looked to my right, where Tommy was seated, busily playing Monster GO. When I glanced back toward my mom, I nodded. "I am. And I have to admit, it's more fun than I thought it would be."

"See, sis. You should listen to me next time I tell you about a game. I know you think I'm just your stupid little brother, but I can teach you a thing or two about life." He smiled smugly as he continued playing the game.

"I'm glad you and Tommy have been able to find something that you're both interested in." Mom paused and then crossed her arms. "But since we're about to eat, I'm going to have to ask you to put your phones away for me. I want to have a nice sit-down dinner with my family."

"Sounds good," I said, as I set my phone on the table.

It took a little bit of persuasion, but finally Tommy did the same thing. Dad popped around the corner and took a seat at the head of the table as Mom laid out the food.

"How is my wonderful family this evening?" he asked, settling in and putting the napkin on his lap.

"Doing well," I said. I felt like I had stepped back in time to my high school days. The feeling wasn't a bad one.

"Fine," Tommy replied, eyeing his phone resting next to him.

"We're great, honey, how are you?" Mom asked. She sat down and smiled around the table.

"I'm okay. Have a long week ahead of me, but I know that it's worth it." He took a bite of steak. "I'm going to put in for a promotion soon, and I'm hoping these extra hours will show the boss that I deserve a managerial position."

"No matter what happens with the promotion, we're all still proud of you," Mom said, setting her knife down with a smile.

It felt just like old times. I was no longer twenty-two. I was somewhere between twelve and eighteen. A child, safe and secure while my parents took care of the world. It was as if I'd stepped back five years in time. Nothing felt like it had changed, even though my world was entirely different.

"Thanks, honey," Dad said. He paused for a moment and brought his attention toward me. "Speaking of work-related things, how's the job hunt coming along, Alicia? Any new leads?"

I chewed up my first bite of steak and then swallowed. I

couldn't tell him that I had wasted the entire day. I'd spent the morning with Jacob and then the afternoon talking with Caroline and playing my new game.

"Nothing yet." It was the only thing I could really say.

"You'll find something," Mom said, before my dad could chime in.

I was sick of getting asked all the time about the job thing. It wasn't like I wasn't looking and it certainly wasn't like I was a child that needed constant reminder. Yet again, the feeling of time travel prevailed.

Luckily, my parents diverted their attention and asked Tommy about his day, which took the spotlight off of me. Meanwhile, my thoughts went to Jacob. Tomorrow couldn't come soon enough. I wanted to see him again. I wanted to talk to him, hear him laugh, kiss him, make him smile, and share our worlds.

We ate our meal and when we were all finished, I leaned back and patted my belly. "I'm stuffed."

"That was really good, Mom," Tommy said.

"Aww, thank you, Tom Tom," she replied, smiling around the table and looking pleased.

"Thank you for the delicious meal, baby," Dad said, as he gazed across the table toward my mother.

They both got up and I watched as they took their plates to the sink. My mom turned on the water and my dad stepped behind her, wrapping his arms around her waist. She giggled and looked over her shoulder at him. They looked into each other's eyes before kissing.

"Gross," Tommy grunted. He had glanced up from his phone just long enough to see the interaction between our parents.

I couldn't have disagreed with Tommy's sentiment more. In fact, the scene made my heart swell. My parents loved each other and they weren't afraid to show it. I had to hand it to them. They definitely knew how to have a successful relationship.

Where Caroline would tell me stories of her parents fighting and threatening divorce, I got to witness the most loving marriage ever. They set a great example of how it should be done and I truly hoped that one day I'd get to experience the same thing.

What I loved most about them is that their love seemed totally authentic. They didn't hug and kiss each other goodbye in the morning because they thought that was what they were *supposed* to do. They did it because they actually felt like showing the affection.

I would love to have someone that treats me as well as my mom gets treated, I thought.

It made me think of how my dad always opened the door for her, held her hand, kissed her cheek and told her he loved her. I didn't have a single memory of the two of them getting in an argument. It just never happened. It felt like a pipe dream that I could ever find anything as amazing as that, but I still had hope. I always had hope.

Tommy elbowed my ribs, forcing me to look away. "What, Tommy?"

"Just wanted to show you the latest monster I caught. It's standing right over there in the living room. If you paid attention for two seconds, you might have noticed."

Sure enough, my phone had been vibrating, and when I picked it up there was a notification from the game. I walked to the living room to catch my monster. The experience points caused me to jump up to another level. Pretty soon and I'd be able to pick a team to play on.

"You're totally addicted, aren't you?" Tommy asked, stepping up beside me.

"No way," I said, though a part of me knew that I was lying.

"Whatever," Tommy replied with a roll of his eyes. "You just want to be able to play with Caroline."

"How did you find out that Caroline started playing?" I asked, surprised that he knew my friend had started playing the game as well.

"Because, I saw her running around the park like a crazy person this morning to try to catch a stupid Fireliz." Tommy laughed. "It was pretty funny, actually."

"Yeah, well, you're right. She got addicted pretty quick, but that hasn't happened to me." I shrugged like I didn't care, but I wasn't actually entirely sure.

"At least this game introduced you to someone cool." Tommy picked up his phone and made a couple of swipes.

"Do you really think he's cool?" I asked, sounding more eager than I intended to.

"Anybody on Team Red is a friend of mine." He put the phone back in his pocket.

"You just like him because he gave you ten dollars." I gave him a gentle push as he laughed.

He smiled. "I can't argue with the truth," he said.

CHAPTER 5

When I woke up the next morning, the first thing that I did was snatch my phone off of the nightstand. Normally, I'd have checked my email or looked to see if I'd gotten any hits on my job search, but instead, I opened up the Monster GO app. I wondered if maybe I was becoming slightly addicted to it, but I still wasn't to the point where I was going to admit it, even to myself.

An update was available on the game and I downloaded it. While it loaded, I realized that for the first time since graduation, I hadn't awoken to my first thought being about finding a job. It was far better to wake up excited to play a game rather than disappointed to not have a job. If nothing else, the game was making my world a little bit brighter and I was glad for it.

When the game restarted, I was surprised to find that the appearance of the game looked a bit different than before. Now, instead of being able to see monsters that were within a one or two block radius, I could zoom out on the map and see my entire town. In addition, if I clicked on a street, the name would appear. The Monster GO world had opened up significantly and there was suddenly so many more areas to play.

This is why I need to find a job where I can create apps or software, I thought. *I was right on the money. This update was exactly what I thought the game needed. Maybe there's a future in app creation for me.*

If only that was enough to get a job. I needed to get up and get ready for the day. Jacob would be at the house soon to pick me up for our morning walk. So I got up, took a quick shower and then changed into my black yoga pants and red tank top. And even though I was getting ready for exercise, I still straightened my hair and put on makeup. It seemed silly, but I wanted to look my absolute best for Jacob.

Once I was ready, I walked downstairs and into the kitchen. My parents were seated at the bar, drinking coffee and eating scrambled eggs. They looked up when I walked in.

"Good morning," Mom said, with her usual smile.

"Morning," I replied. "How are you two doing?"

"Doing well," Dad said. "You look like you're ready for a run or something."

I shrugged. "Not a run, but definitely a walk."

"I'm glad you're getting out," he said. "You've seemed a lot happier the last couple of days. Maybe this morning exercise thing is exactly what you needed."

"I think you're right," I agreed. I stood there for a moment, awkwardly shuffling my feet on the floor. I had put off telling them about my "friend" Jacob for a few days, but I couldn't keep it a secret any longer. He'd be there in a few minutes to pick me up and it would be easier to just introduce him now than try and explain him later.

"I have a friend coming over to go on a walk with me," I finally managed to get out.

"Oh, really? Is Caroline is coming by?" Mom asked. She put a couple of dishes in the sink and waited for me to answer.

"No, a different friend." I wanted to act casual, but it wasn't easy. I wasn't entirely sure where my nerves came from, especially with something as simple as introducing my parents to a new friend, but introducing a male friend was never simple.

"Who is she?" Dad asked, not looking up from his morning paper.

"It's not a she." I corrected him. "*His* name is Jacob. I met him in the park a few days ago."

Dad stopped reading and looked over his paper. He didn't say anything, but I could tell he was trying to remember where he last put his shotgun. He liked to clean it whenever guys came over.

"When will he be here?" Mom asked. She looked excited. There was a gleam in her eye as she spoke. More than likely, she was already assuming Jacob to be a potential boyfriend for me even though she hadn't met him yet.

"Any minute," I said, glancing down at my watch. The sooner he got here, the sooner I could get out of here.

"Is he cute?" Mom asked, her lips curling up into an even wider smile.

"Moooooom." I placed my hands onto my hips and cocked my head to the side, doing my best to impersonate an annoyed teenager. Mom just laughed.

"Well?" she pressed, not letting me off the hook. "Is he cute or not?"

"A little," I replied. I tried not to smile, but I couldn't stop myself. "He's a little bit cute."

"Uh huh," Mom replied with a knowing grin. She winked at me before pouring herself another cup of coffee. "When do we get to meet him?"

"Eventually," I promised. "He's just a friend, Mom. I'm sure you'll meet him soon."

"I hope so," she replied. "I haven't seen you look this happy since you got here. If nothing else, I like this guy for that."

"Me too," Dad agreed. I turned to him, slightly surprised.

"Even though he's keeping me from my job hunting?" I asked, crossing my arms and preparing myself for my dad's disappointment.

"Honey, I just want you to be happy," Dad replied, setting his paper down. "I want you to have a career that you're proud of and that lets you live your life. I don't care about the job search, just that you get where you need to go."

My arms fell from their defensive posture. "Thanks, Daddy."

Dad picked up his paper again. "Oh look, McMurray's Hardware is hiring..."

"Thanks, Dad," I replied quickly and hurried out of the kitchen. I could hear Dad chuckling as I ran out the front door to meet Jacob.

CHAPTER 6

*J*acob was poised to ring the doorbell as I opened the door. He jumped slightly, but smiled widely as I stepped out. He had on his glasses today, which I found out helped him with computer work.

"You forgot to take off your glasses," I reminded him as I closed the door behind me.

"Thank you," he replied, taking them off and putting them in his pocket. "I was working before I came. It was a busy work day today. You look great, by the way."

I loved the way his eyes twinkled when he looked at me. I felt like I was the center of the universe when he looked at me like that, and it made my stomach do happy somersaults.

"Which direction should we go?" he asked, taking my hand in his and leading me down the driveway. I liked the way his hand felt wrapped around mine.

I looked to my left, where the park with the fountain was located, then I turned to my right. A couple of miles down the road in that direction was William's Park. I hadn't been there in a long time and I kind of wanted to see what it looked like after all these years. Besides, I thought Jacob might like it since it wouldn't be as crowded as the fountain.

"How about William's Park?" I asked, taking a step to the right.

"I'm new here, so you'll have to take the lead. I don't have any idea where it is. But sure, sounds like a fun little adventure," he said with a smile.

"You'll love it. It's nicer than the other park in town. It's a little ways away, but as long as you're ready for it, let's go," I told him.

We turned right and walked up the street, past my neighbor's houses. Our fingers were interlocked the entire time. I had feared there would be some awkwardness between us after our kiss the day before, but there was none of that. It just felt natural to be around him.

"How was your night?" he asked, as we turned the corner out of the neighborhood and onto a dirt trail that would eventually lead to William's Park.

"It was fine. Just hung out with my friend, Caroline." I looked over at him, squinting slightly in the sun. "How was yours?"

"Nothing too exciting. I pretty much just unpacked some boxes all evening and worked on some new updates for my latest project. And for dinner, I ate macaroni and cheese, since I didn't have any food in my fridge at all," he said. "It was kind of sad. I haven't eaten mac and cheese and called it a meal since college."

"You need to go grocery shopping, silly," I told him with a laugh. "I'm not sure how long you can live off of mac and cheese, but I doubt it's very long."

"Do you want to help me with that?" he said, as we continued our walk along the dirt path. The only sound other than the two of us was birds and the soft summer breeze. "I absolutely loathe grocery shopping. I always intend to buy a bunch of things to stock up on, but as soon as I have one meal in my cart, I'm ready to leave."

"Well, I *love* grocery shopping," I said with a laugh. "So, I'll make it fun for both of us."

"Let's do that soon," he said. "Or else I'm going to starve."

We walked quietly for a little while and I just savored the moment. The air was crisp and clean with the promise of heat later in the day. The smell of vegetation along the dirt path brought a wave of nostalgia. It reminded me of when I was younger. Tommy was still a little kid then, and would come with me to William's Park to try to catch frogs near the river.

"Have you been playing Monster GO at all?" Jacob asked, drawing me from my memories.

"Actually, I have." I pulled out my phone and opened up the app. "You know what's really funny though?"

"What's that?" he asked, pulling out his so we could play together.

"Do you remember the other day when you asked what I thought would make the game better?"

"Yeah, I do." He cocked his head to the side as he remembered. "You mentioned something about wanting to be able to see a larger area on the map to make it easier to find monsters."

"Yes, exactly. Well, guess what?" I passed my phone over to him. "Looks like they made the change. Must have been a pretty good idea, because I wasn't the only one to see the need for improvement."

"Maybe you have a future in game development," he said. "It was a really good idea."

"You never know," I said, slipping my phone back into my pocket. I tried to keep the discouragement out of my voice. "I'd sure love that, but I'm having a hard time visual-izing it ever happening. The job search has gone nowhere. I haven't even gotten a callback on anything yet."

"Just keep at it," he said, giving my hand a squeeze. "You're obviously smart and clearly beautiful. There's two things that I don't have, and I've been able to somehow make things happen for me. There's not a doubt in my mind that things will work out for you."

I smiled at the compliment. I couldn't remember the last time someone called me both smart and beautiful in the same sentence. "You're too sweet," I said. "But you're smart, too."

For the next fifteen minutes or so, we just walked and talked. We shared stories about college and our families. I learned that his parents lived on the East Coast, so he didn't get to see them as often as he would have liked. They sounded like they were wonderful people and I found myself hoping that I would someday get to meet them.

A few times, our phones buzzed in our pockets and we pulled them out to catch a monster or two. They were ones that I already had, though, so I didn't get too excited. I was more interested in being present with Jacob and less with the game.

"Come here. I want to show you something," I said, pulling on Jacob's hand as we entered the park.

I walked quickly across the grass with Jacob right behind me. We darted off of the main path and into some nearby bushes. They were so thick that if I hadn't known about the river there, I probably would have just ran right by it.

"Where are taking me?" he asked, followed by a chuckle. "I can hardly fit through here."

"Just push through here."

"I'm not even going to say it," Jacob replied, laughter echoing through his words.

After clearing the bushes, and getting snagged on just about every branch possible, we stepped into a clearing alongside the river. When Jacob popped out, he had pieces of grass and debris all over his clothes.

"You're a mess." I carefully reached out and took a blade of grass from his hair. It felt like such an intimate gesture that I immediately blushed. I didn't pull away, though.

"This is beautiful," he said, looking around the area and thankfully not at my blush.

The stream in front of us was crystal clear. It was only a couple of feet wide, small enough so that it didn't attract much attention, but still beautiful. It was my own secret place. It was one of the only places in William's park that not a lot of people knew about, if any. Tommy and I had been coming to the exact spot since we were kids. It appeared to have been untouched by anyone else.

"You like it?" I asked, suddenly nervous for his approval. I'd never brought anyone here before, but it had felt right to bring him.

"How did you ever even find this spot?" he replied, looking over at the bushes. "I don't think anyone would ever even look here."

"Tommy and I used to be a lot smaller and those bushes weren't quite as thick," I explained. "We found it one summer after a flood cleared a lot of the river out. There's a dam now, so you don't have to worry about it happening again."

"It's a secret oasis," he said. He turned to face me, his eyes still wandering and taking in all the beauty around us. "This is amazing, Alicia."

"Thank you," I said quietly. "I'm really glad you like it."

"Do you come out here a lot?" His gaze returned to me, but his smile remained the same.

"Not in a long time," I admitted. "I'm pretty sure the last time I was here was before I moved away for college."

We stepped over to a downed tree that laid along the river's edge and kicked off our shoes before sitting on the tree. We dipped our feet in the cool water, which sent a shiver up my body. It felt refreshing, though, too. It made me feel truly at home for some reason.

"Is this your favorite spot in town?" Jacob asked. "If you had to choose one spot, this would be the one?"

"Yeah, I think so. It just has so many memories for me. This entire park does, actually." I smiled as I remembered. "On the weekends we used to play volleyball. Sometimes my dad would set it up so we could play horseshoes in the sand on the opposite side of the park from where we're at now. This place holds a lot of great memories for me."

"I can see why," he said. He kicked his feet in the stream, making tiny ripples go out into the water. "It might be the prettiest place I've seen since I moved to town. I mean the city is nice, but this spot just feels special for some reason."

"I'm glad you like it." I scooted a little closer to Jacob.

He wrapped his arm around my lower back and pulled me close. Our hips were pressed together and I leaned my head against his shoulder. The river flowed across our feet. I dug my toes into the sand, loving the way my feet were cold but the rest of me was going hot. It made me both nervous and excited.

"It's weird," I whispered. "I feel like I know you, even though we've only known each other for a little while."

"I've been thinking that same thing," he said. He made small circles on my back with his fingers. "I believe that's what made me want to talk to you when I first saw you a few days ago. You felt familiar to me. It sounds crazy, but..."

"It doesn't sound crazy at all," I said, cutting his words short. "It's how I feel, too."

I looked up at him and our eyes locked. The blues of his eyes deepened and pulled me into him. There was such kindness and warmth to their depths. He smiled and it caused me to melt.

"You're so beautiful," he said, shaking his head in slow disbelief. "Where did you come from? A fairyland?"

I chuckled. "I've wondered the same thing about you."

He leaned in and kissed me. His soft lips pressed against mine, momentarily taking my breath away. I loved the way he tasted. He used just enough pressure as he leaned in. Then he pulled away, gently. He teased me like this, pecking his lips forward and then leaning back a bit. The ebb and flow of the dance turned me on. I was practically panting after a few minutes. I couldn't believe how a kiss could be so sweet one moment and enticingly hot the next.

I pulled away, catching my breath for a moment. I was barely able to catch two breaths before he kissed me again. This time, he didn't pull away at all, though. We opened our lips and our tongues dashed in and out of each other's mouths.

I wanted to kiss him for the rest of the day. Time didn't matter anymore. His fingers caressed my skin, sending spirals of desire down into my fingertips. I didn't know how he did it, but every touch, every kiss, made me hungry for more.

We were all alone here. I didn't have to worry about Tommy showing up or anyone walking by. I had been thinking of him all night, wanting to kiss him. Wanting to do so much more than *just* kiss him.

Without breaking our kiss, I crawled over top of him, straddling his lap. We fit like two pieces of a puzzle. I moaned softly without breaking the kiss. My body took over. Thoughts were a thing that didn't exist in that moment. I wanted him on a different level. I wanted to taste him and feel him, deeply and completely.

Jacob's hands drifted until they landed on the side of my legs, almost to my butt. He pulled away, though, looking me in the eyes. His pupils had dilated and there was a lust in his eyes that I could only describe as carnal.

"I want you so bad right now," he groaned, his voice rough with desire.

"Me too," I whispered. I rocked my hips gently to accentuate my point.

"But, I don't want whatever is between us to be just about sex," he said. His eyes met mine and I could see the honesty and honor in them. "There's something amazing about you, and I don't want to rush things."

"What do you mean?" I asked. My words were still paced between heavy breathing.

"I want you right now, but I know that if we have sex before getting to know each other a little bit more, then I'll regret it. It won't be as special." He gave me a half smile. "We haven't even had a proper date and I want to give you that at least. You deserve it."

My body was craving his. Every primal bone in my body wanted to feel him within me, but I couldn't deny that I absolutely loved the respect he was showing me. He made it clear that sleeping with me wasn't his only priority in our spending time. I loved that. I loved that so much.

"A date, huh?" I asked with a smile, not quite ready to move off of him.

"Yeah, what do you think?" he asked. He blushed slightly with nerves, and it made my heart flutter.

"I think that sounds pretty nice," I admitted. I bit my lip. "What did you have in mind?"

Jacob looked up thoughtfully. "I have some ideas. Why don't you let me just make it a surprise?"

"A surprise?" I asked. "I guess I could get behind that. But you need to tell me how I should dress for it. I don't want to end up wearing sweat pants or something."

"Wear something really nice," he said, with a smile. "Do you have a dress that you never get to wear? Something special."

"I've got the perfect thing." I thought about the little black dress in my closet that had been given to me as a birthday gift from my aunt a few years prior. I'd gotten to wear it exactly once, and had been looking for an excuse to wear it ever since. It was the fanciest article of clothing that I owned and it sounded like it was exactly what Jacob had in mind.

"Good," he said. A wicked grin crossed his face. "Oh, and one more thing."

My eyebrows rose. "What's that?"

"Let's make this a phone-free date," he said. "I know that we've been playing Monster GO quite a bit together and it's a lot of fun, but I want to have an evening with you that doesn't involve any distractions. What do you say?"

My smile couldn't have gotten any wider if I'd tried. "It sounds amazing."

He grinned. "Good."

"But, just because we are taking our time doesn't mean I want to stop kissing you," I informed him. I was still on his lap and had no intention of moving.

Jacob leaned forward and kissed me again. He tasted like

sunshine. All I could hear around us was the sound of the babbling stream and the wind in the leaves. I couldn't have asked for a more perfect moment.

"When did you want to go on this surprise date?" I asked, as soon as we broke our kiss.

"How about Friday night?" he asked after a moment. "I'll pick you up at six."

"Sounds like a plan," I replied, my heart already beating fast. I couldn't wait to see what he had in mind. "I'll be ready."

"Me too," he said, grinning like a kid before Christmas. "It's going to be amazing."

I doubted his excitement could even come close to matching mine. I couldn't wait to see what kind of surprise he had in store for me.

I started to slide off his lap, to take my place just sitting next to him again. He caught my waist in his hands, and held me still.

"Just where do you think you're going?" he asked, his voice low and seductive.

I frowned slightly. "You said you wanted to wait..."

He chuckled, throaty and deep. "I said I wanted to wait for sex," he clarified. "We still have all our clothes on."

He rocked into me, letting me feel his desire as he leaned forward and kissed my neck. The soft caress of his lips against the sensitive bare skin made me shiver and my core heat.

"So, if we keep our clothes on, we don't have to stop?" I asked, my eyes fluttering as he kept kissing my throat and teasing me with his touch.

"That's right," he murmured.

I found myself suddenly wishing I had worn less cloth-ing. "I can handle that," I said, rocking my hips to match his.

My whole body reacted as he groaned and bit down on my shoulder.

"You're going to make me regret wanting to be honorable," he groaned.

"Waiting makes it better," I promised. "And I'll make it worth the wait."

Jacob looked up at me, his blue eyes full of dark desire. "I know you will." He grinned, and continued to tease me as much as I was teasing him.

CHAPTER 7

I'd taken a shower and begun getting ready at four o'clock, a full two hours before Jacob was set to pick me up. I straightened my hair, painted my fingers and toes and even applied a thin layer of nude lipstick.

Wear something really nice, he'd said, the words playing over in my head in the exact tone that he'd spoken them. I bit my lip as I stared in the mirror. It wasn't a concern over my dress that was making me anxious, it was the entire statement as a whole. The fact that he'd prefaced our date with an expectation of, '*really nice.*'

I certainly didn't mind 'really nice,' in fact it was exciting, but that same excitement had been twirling in my stomach since breakfast and had now grown into a flurry of anxious anticipation. I had no idea where or what we were doing. The nicest restaurant in town didn't really qualify as a "dressing up" kind of place, so that meant we had to be going to at least the next town over.

My belly felt empty yet somehow full, with weightless pulses of energy and giddy eagerness. I felt the same sensation in my fingers as I applied the finishing touches to my makeup. I had no idea what was going to happen next or where in the world we might end up.

Jacob had turned me into a little kid again. Between the Monster game and the persistent feeling of joyful jitters, there was no doubt about it. He'd introduced a new sort of spark that left me eager at the start of each day and cheerfully content in the evening. Even my mind pumped with a different chemistry than before, one of pleasant optimism and assurance. He was a beautiful substance, and I was hooked.

I checked my image in the mirror one more time. My hair fell fairly straight while still maintaining a light wave, a feat I was rarely able to achieve. Generally my hair was obnoxiously uncooperative, a programming glitch that induced a migraine when I tried to fix it. But today, luck was on my side, and I didn't take it for granted. I added a thin and diagonal braid to help pull my bangs back.

I continued to watch the clock, even though I'd allowed myself plenty of time. Each and every minute marking another step closer to Jacob. It was just after five-thirty when Tommy knocked and then bounded through my door before I'd even answered.

"Hey, guess what?" he said, and I spun around again.

"What?" I asked, just grateful I had put clothes on. We were going to have to have a discussion about him knocking sometime soon. He wasn't a five year old little boy who didn't know better anymore.

He extended his hand holding his phone. "Look! Now there's a Monster Stop at the end of our block, at the park."

"Oh, wow," I said, slightly surprised and a little excited. "When did that show up?"

"I just noticed it today," he said. He sighed like the

weight of the world had been lifted from his shoulders. "*Finally* we've got one close to our house."

"Yeah, no kidding," I agreed. "It will be nice not to have to go so far all the time."

"Seems like they finally listened to me." He smiled smugly, as if he had been the reason the game had added the stop.

"Well, if it makes you feel any better, if *I* was the one making the app I would have listened to you a long time ago," I said. "I would've hooked you up."

I winked at him and then turned around again.

"I know you would. It certainly took them long enough," he said. "I wish you were working for them. Then stuff would actually get done."

"They're probably off somewhere counting their piles of money," I said. "I'm not sure checking user recommendations is exactly at the top of their priority list."

"ALICIA, someone just pulled into the driveway," my mom yelled up from the stairs not five minutes after Tommy left.

Jacob's here, I answered her in my head. I couldn't have wiped the smile off my face with sandblaster. I couldn't wait for this evening to start.

My father was sitting in the corner of the couch with his feet propped up, reading a copy of The Wall Street Journal, his regular and favorite choice of post-work leisure. He was the first to speak as I came down the stairs, glancing up and above the top edge of his magazine cover.

"You look nice," he said with a warm smile.

"Thanks, Daddy." I grinned at him, pleased with the compliment.

His comment drew my mother from around the kitchen corner. "Oh sweetie, you look gorgeous," she said with a smile that rivaled my father's.

"You guys going somewhere nice?" My father peered over the top of his paper at me.

"That's what I was told," I replied.

"Do you know where?" my mother asked, an excited smile on her face.

"Not yet," I said. "It's a *surprise.*"

"Ah," my father coughed. "Guy knows what he's doing," he said and offered a pointed look towards my mother.

Mom rolled her eyes. "I have *never* liked surprises."

"Oh, that's what they always say," he said, giving me a wink.

"But that never stopped your father," my mother finished her sentence, leaving her stare on my dad for a moment before turning to me. I wondered what kind of surprise he could have given her that was creating this kind of reaction.

"You know you liked it," Dad replied, going back to his paper.

Mom just rolled her eyes again and shook her head. "Have a good time, sweetie."

"Thanks, Mom." I grinned at her and headed toward the door. "I have my key, so don't worry about waiting up for me."

"Of course, dear," Mom replied, giving me an all too knowing look. I simply shook my head and left the room before my dad could comment. Jacob was on his way to the door as I stepped out.

"Oh, you're not even gonna make me knock?" He smiled and looked me up and down. Twice. "You look absolutely stunning."

"You said wear something nice," I said, shrugging. My cheeks flushed in a way that formed a smile without me trying.

"I expected your beautiful self in a nice dress, but you exceeded my expectations," he said as we embraced in a hug.

My head settled into his shoulder and immediately I could smell his cologne, an aroma of a post-rain-like scent blended with a crisp masculine fragrance. I savored his smell like it was a nearby flower until our hug ended and the scent became lost in the surrounding air.

"You look very, *very* nice as well," I said and even allowed myself to look him up and down without feeling pretentious. No, it felt much more like pausing to admire a fine painting.

He had slicked his dark hair back, which made him look sophisticated. It was amazing how his fine suit transformed him into someone worthy of a magazine cover. He grinned, crinkling the corners of his eyes. He wore his glasses this evening, which I thought made him look smart. They accented his eyes and fit his face well.

He led me to his car and opened my passenger side door, gesturing with his hand to invite me in. I felt like a princess, or a celebrity. Those types of people had doors opened for them, not me. It was a wonderful feeling.

"I was kind of hoping to get in a little Monster GO with your brother before we left," he said, his right hand gripping the top of the leather steering wheel as we sped down the road to the highway. "It's too bad you beat me to the door."

"Really?" I said, looking over at him. He grinned back at me and immediately I felt foolish for sounding so surprised. I laughed as I realized he was just teasing me.

"No, I'm kidding. No phones, remember?" he said and

lifted up the center compartment between us. "I've got my mine buried in here, and that's where it's going to stay for the night."

I took my phone out of my small clutch and tossed it into the center compartment with his.

"There," I announced.

"There," he echoed, wearing a proud smile as he closed the compartment and rested his elbow on it.

We drove in companionable silence until we reached the highway.

"So where are we going?" I was so curious it had taken everything I had not to ask the second I saw him. I was impressed that I had managed to make it to the highway before asking.

"It's a surprise," he reminded me.

I put on my biggest pout, pushing out my bottom lip as far as I could and giving him big, sad, puppy-dog eyes.

He laughed. My pout was having no effect on him.

"If I told you now, it wouldn't be a surprise anymore," he explained.

"How about I just act surprised?" I said. "And I'll be surprised here, in the car."

"Nah. Doesn't work that way," he said, shaking his head. "That'd be like us getting halfway through a scary movie and me all of a sudden telling you how it ends. Besides, we're almost there."

"Really?" I asked. I peered through my window and tried to run through the list of nearby restaurants. We were well out of my small town, but since I hadn't been paying attention to which direction we were going, I wasn't sure quite where we were.

"Well, comparatively speaking. We're closer to dinner

than we were this morning," he said with a chuckle. "But, driving wise we're maybe, eh, ten, fifteen minutes away."

"If you say so," I replied. I slouched back in my seat and crossed my arms. I wasn't really angry. I couldn't be with him there. There was something about him talking to me, something about his presence that was both soothing and captivating. It was the thing I missed most when we were apart.

He laughed and asked me about my day. Our conversation was easy and flowed as I lost track of how long we were in the car. Those ten or fifteen minutes felt like seconds.

We were engaged in a serious debate about the merits of different computer programming codes when we pulled onto flat cobblestone that circled around a fountain and small garden. We rounded the circle halfway, stopping at the door of the restaurant.

"We've gotta get out here," he said as I gave him a confused look. "They valet at this place."

"Oh, wow," I whispered to myself before stepping out the door. This *was* fancy.

The restaurant's entrance was grand in every aspect of the word. Designed to imitate a sort of Victorian-era mansion, the place was long and wide and looked to be three stories tall with triangular contours that jutted out peaking and blending into the shingled roof. The outer walls were a natural looking gray, but had vines and various flowers growing up their sides. Windows and balconies lined the building, and I could easily imagine Romeo climbing up to one to meet his Juliet.

A thin stone path lead from the cobblestone driveway up to a beautiful deck. The deck was wide enough to collect assorted groups of guests, all conversing while sipping from drinks. I stole a glance at the patrons on the deck and was extremely glad Jacob had suggested a *nice* dress.

Jacob offered me his arm as we stepped inside the beautiful restaurant. The hostess quickly greeted us and we didn't even have to wait for a table.

I was trying to contain my wonder, but as we followed our host to the table I couldn't help but comment, "This place is *really* nice."

"You like it?" Jacob asked. He unconsciously pulled at his tie, revealing that he was more nervous than he appeared.

"It's beautiful," I said. "I kind of can't believe it."

I felt Jacob's hand against my lower back, guiding me to my place at the table. I wanted to turn around and produce a smile crazy enough to match the butterflies in my stomach, but it just didn't feel right to do so in such a fancy place.

"I wanted to take you somewhere really nice," he said as took the chair directly across from me.

"This is," I paused to search for the right word, "this is... I don't even know. This place is absolutely incredible."

He smiled back at me and held it as my eyes wandered about the interior.

Inside, the restaurant didn't lose any element of its charm. Massive chandeliers hung from the ceiling, illuminating the stone walls and the engraved designs throughout.

"Have you ever been here before?" I asked after finding my way back to his gaze.

"No, actually I haven't. But I have a good friend that came here once to propose to his fiancée," he said. "I guess it'll be a first time for both of us."

"What a nice place to get proposed to," I said. "Lucky girl."

"*I'm* lucky getting to take you here."

I knew I was blushing again and there was nothing I could do to stop it. He was so charming. I brought my smile into my menu as I lifted it up, immediately noting its clean and professional layout and the meal options. *And* the prices.

I'd never even seen a menu this expensive. I was fairly sure just sitting at a table cost money.

"Let's split the bill," I said more sheepishly than I'd intended. There was an uneasy feeling of guilt that I had been unable to push out from my chest since arriving at the fancy entrance and the menu had only heightened the sentiment to an uncomfortable level.

Jacob shook his head. "Nope. Dinner's on me."

"I don't know if I feel right about that," I said. "This place is, well, it's beyond incredible. And the valet. It can't be cheap."

"It doesn't really matter either way, though," he said, waving his hand like it was nothing. "It's the place I wanted to take you."

"We could have gone to somewhere," I paused again to pick my words carefully, "somewhere a little more *normal.*"

"Or we could've come here," he said. "And since I was the one picking the surprise, *this* is what I picked."

"I'm not going to let you surprise me anymore," I said, regrettably realizing I sounded too much like my mother had when I left for dinner.

"Oh yes you are," he said with a grin and a glimmer in his eye. And I realized he sounded something like my father, his words nestling their way tenderly into my chest, soothing my concern. I could hear the phrase my father had spoken blending into the moment in my head; *guy knows what he's doing.*

The server arrived and after welcoming us to our first

visit he pointed up and down the menu, eager to inform and delve into their many specialties.

"What's your favorite?" Jacob asked, frowning slightly at the menu. "Everything looks so good."

"I have too many to count," the waiter replied with a laugh. "We make such great food here. But, my favorite would have to be the New York Sirloin with shredded lobster and lemon."

Jacob smiled and nodded back at him. "I'll have to think about it."

"Of course. Can I start you both with some drinks for right now?" the waiter asked. "It will give you a little bit longer to look over the menu."

"That sounds perfect. How about your wines?" Jacob asked, flipping through the wine menu. It was several pages long.

"What do you usually like?" the waiter asked and after a pause I realized he was looking at me.

"Oh, I like reds," I said, feeling slightly like I had to recover from my momentary hesitation.

Jacob nodded, grinning at my awkwardness. "What's your best red?" he asked.

"I recommend this one," the waiter replied, pointing to a French wine on the menu. "It's not *too* sweet, but it isn't as strong as some reds can be. Really a great all around blend. And it pairs really well with the sirloin and shredded lobster," he said, with a knowing smile.

Jacob looked at me as if to subtly ask my approval. "Does that sound good to you?" he asked.

"I'm sure it's excellent," I said, feeling a little overwhelmed. My wine selection skills were more of the twist cap variety.

"We'll start with that for now," Jacob said. "A bottle, please."

"Yes, sir. You won't be disappointed," the waiter assured us. "And are you thinking about any appetizers this evening?"

"How about one order of the pear bruschetta with pecans and blue cheese?" Jacob said while once again eyeing for my approval. I nodded.

"Another great choice." The waiter smiled and then hurried off to start our order.

"Make sure you order exactly what you want," Jacob told me. "Don't even look at the price. Pretend they're made up numbers or something."

I chuckled nervously. The numbers next to the dishes were basically made up. Especially for an unemployed graduate. "I'll try."

"Please order what you'd like." Jacob reached out and touched my hand. "I can afford it. I wouldn't have brought you here if I couldn't."

"So you're not just trying to show off?" I asked, smiling at him.

He laughed and pushed his glasses up the bridge of his nose. "Well, maybe a little."

Our waiter returned after a moment, showing Jacob the bottle of wine before skillfully opening it and pouring just a taste into a glass. Jacob swirled the wine and took his time tasting it. I wondered if he actually knew what he was doing, or if he was just really good at pretending to know how to taste a wine.

"It's very good," Jacob announced. The waiter smiled and quickly took our orders before leaving the both of us with full glasses of the dark red wine.

I waited until the waiter left to take a long taste of my

wine, since I really didn't know what I was doing. It *was* really good, better than any wine I'd had in a long time.

"Do you like it?" Jacob asked, carefully watching my reaction.

"I love it," I said. "It's *really* good." Subconsciously I lifted my glass again for another sip. It was starting to settle and warm my throat. The deep taste lingered on the edge of my tongue and I thought of Caroline. The wine was exceptionally better than anything we'd downed in school late at night while binge watching HGTV.

"Good." He grinned and leaned forward, placing his chin on his hands. "So, tell me about yourself." A smirk in the corner of his lips told me he was joking before it became a full smile.

I laughed, searching for a witty rebuttal. "As this is our first date, I'll tell you that I like long walks on the beach and getting caught in the rain."

"That sounds about right for first date conversation." Jacob laughed. It was rich and comfortable, and something about it made my soul happy. "I'm glad I'm finally able to take you on a real date instead of a Monster GO walk or something."

"Thanks for taking me out," I said. "I'm beyond happy to be here with you."

"I'm just glad you agreed to come," he replied. "I was half afraid you wouldn't."

"Why wouldn't I?" I asked, puzzled.

"Let's just say that the last time I was this excited about a date, it didn't go so well," Jacob said, taking a sip of his wine.

"You can't just leave me hanging with a story like that," I told him. I was rather flattered that he was excited about our date.

He blushed slightly. "The last time I was this excited

about a date, I was thirteen and she was a year older than me and on the cheerleading team."

"Sounds like you were batting above your league," I remarked with a smile.

"Way out of my league," he agreed with a chuckle.

I paused. "The last time you were this excited about a date you were thirteen?"

"Yeah." He looked down at his menu and then fixed his tie. "I've been excited about dates, but never this excited."

My heart melted.

"I'm excited too," I admitted. "But, are you as cute now as you were then?"

"I was such a ridiculous looking kid," he said with a laugh. "Crazy hair, huge glasses, braces, and terribly scrawny."

"Glasses and braces, huh?" I smiled at him. "But you're like a solid six-foot now, so you probably weren't really that short."

"Oh no, I was short," he assured me. "I'm six-foot now, but I probably grew about three feet in college. I was *tiny* then."

"How short are we talking?" I said, muffling my giggle as I spoke.

"I bet you I was probably five-five when I graduated. *Maybe* shorter," he said with a shake of his head.

"No way." I took another sip of my wine, thoroughly enjoying myself. I liked hearing about his life. I wanted to know everything about him. I wanted to know where he came from and how he got here and everything in between.

"Oh yeah. Better believe it," he said. "And that was *gradu-ation.* I was probably five-foot going into high school."

"Oh dear," I said, trying to picture a more miniature Jacob. "I think even I was taller than that."

"I'm sure you were," he said, amusement dancing on his face and in his eyes. "I think just about the whole school was."

"Wow. That's kind of rough," I said while trying to scale back the appearance of my delight, though if we weren't in a nice restaurant I'd already be cracking up.

"Yeah, it was *a lot* of fun," he said, smiling but dripping with sarcasm. "It was a great confidence boost for little Jacob; new kid, coming into a big new school, trying out for the freshman basketball team feeling like the hoop was too tall for me to see."

"You tried out for basketball?" I said. "You couldn't have thought that was a good idea."

"Oh, young Jacob had an abundance of ideas that he thought were good at one time that later proved to be disastrous. Basketball was one," he said. "Swim team was another."

"Swim team, huh?" I asked.

"Oh yes, swim team," he said. "Good ol' swim team. That lasted a little longer than basketball though. They actually let me pretend to participate with that for a little while."

"So you weren't destined to be the next Michael Phelps?"

"I remember thinking, *yeah, I like swimming. Pools are fun. Maybe I can do this.* Nope. Turns out I wasn't real good at the whole, stroke, kick, hold-your-breath kind of thing. Or diving. Wasn't great at that either. I liked cannonballs, but apparently diving required some level of skill above my threshold." He paused and smiled. "So yeah, if you exclude that stuff then I was great at swimming."

We both laughed. It was the kind of laugh that makes the world brighter. It wasn't the polite conversation laugh, but the kind that only people who understand one another can share.

It was then that our food arrived. We took a moment to each taste our meals before continuing the conversation as if we had never left off.

"Young Jacob wasn't exactly cut out for athletics," he said. "Luckily, I realized that before giving the football team a go."

I laughed, imagining a small, five-foot Jacob running under the weight of his pads.

"But why?" I said, smiling gently at him. "You could have been the next NFL star and now you'll never know."

"Oh, *I know,*" he said. "Kind of like how I know that if I were to light myself on fire right now, it'd hurt like all hell. It's one of those things you don't *really* need to experience before you know."

"So now you're comparing athletics to the pain of being lit on fire?" I teased.

"Eh, I don't know if that's fair," he said, thoughtfully. "Athletics might be worse."

I loved laughing with him and it was so easy. There was something about him that lifted my stomach into my chest until I was floating, propelled by his every word, his every syllable. He was beautiful, his eyes were enchanting, his style refined and his smile mesmerizing. But above all, he was authentic.

Never had I met someone that could so comfortably make fun of himself while still maintaining a confident charisma. His authenticity coated every word he spoke and it pooled into a genuine personality that seemed almost tangible. Everything he said or did was *him* in his purest form.

As we finished up, there was a bit of wine still left in the bottle.

"Can I top you off?" he asked. "Guess we might as well finish this."

"Is there enough for both of us?" I asked, eyeing the bottle carefully. I was comfortably relaxed, but I didn't want to get into tipsy territory.

"I guess we'll see when I'm done pouring," he said, and poured the remainder of the bottle into my glass. "Oh, bummer."

I smirked at him. "You did that on purpose."

"Maybe." He grinned. "Take your time and enjoy it. I'm in good company."

I took a small sip. The wine was so good I was secretly glad I got to have more.

"How's the job search going?" he asked.

"Oh, man. I'm glad you refilled my wine glass," I said and let out a wry chuckle. "The job search is going about as fast as a dead horse."

"That well, huh?" he asked, sounding almost as disappointed as I did. "What about that internship? The one with ZephTech?"

"I haven't heard anything yet," I told him. I was surprised, almost stunned that he'd remembered the name.

"I wish you the best of luck," he replied. He frowned slightly before speaking. "I've heard that ZephTech is intense and not for everyone."

"That's true," I agreed. "But it's what I've wanted since I found out about the company. I like hard work, so I think I'll do okay. That is, if I even get it."

"I think you can do just about anything." Jacob reached out and took my hand. "You just have to wait for the right job to come along. It'll happen. I promise."

I believed him. It was strange, but I believed him. When he said it, I felt like it might actually be true and not just a platitude that people would say to make me feel better. For the first time in weeks, I felt like I might be moving in the right direction.

"Thank you," I told him, meaning it completely. "If I get it, you'll have to show me around Silicon Valley, since you've been there."

Jacob's smile faltered.

"What's wrong?" I asked. "Is something wrong with seeing me in Silicon Valley?"

"I hate Silicon Valley. It's why I left." He paused, carefully thinking before speaking. "I don't think I'll ever go back there. Not for a long time, at least."

"Oh." My heart sank a little. I rather liked the idea of Jacob and me working together out there, but the tone of his voice made it very clear that wasn't going to happen.

"But, I would happily meet you somewhere nearby," he promised, reaching out for my hand. "Like San Francisco or Monterrey. Monterrey is beautiful."

I did my best to smile. "I probably won't get it anyway," I said trying to shrug off my disappointment.

"You're going to get something even better," he promised. "I know it."

Jacob paid the bill. He made sure that I wasn't even able to sneak a peek at it, even though I could do the math well enough. This meal probably cost more than my groceries for two weeks did, but I had definitely enjoyed it.

Together we walked hand in hand out the door to wait for his car to be valeted. The delivery of the bill had reintroduced my feelings of guilt, and I watched shamefully as Jacob slid his credit card into the leather folder. Again, I'd wanted to offer to pay, to contribute in some way, but he'd remained positive as he left the payment, almost as if he hardly even noticed the expense, and I didn't want to change that by broaching the subject again.

As we stood outside the night air was humid but cool and soft, a nice change from the controlled climate inside the restaurant. Jacob dropped my hand and reached to wrap his arm around me. I loved the way his heat wrapped around me, and even though the night air was cool, I barely noticed.

I wanted anything but for the night to end. It had gone by way too fast. I didn't even want to see his car pulled around again. Had it disappeared entirely and stranded us there at the restaurant, I wouldn't have minded in the slightest.

The car pulled up. The valet beat Jacob to opening the door for me this time, but I still felt pampered. I reluctantly got into the car, sad that even a portion of our evening was coming to a close.

"You enjoy your dinner?" Jacob asked after a comfortable moment of silence as we drove.

"It was amazing," I said and returned his smile. "I think that was the nicest place I've ever eaten."

"I'm glad you liked it," he replied. "I was afraid it might have been a little over the top."

I smiled. "Maybe a little bit. don't even know what to say because 'thank you' doesn't seem like enough."

"You don't have to say anything," he said. "The pleasure was all mine."

"Okay, I owe you then. My treat next time," I said.

"That's a great segue into my next point," he said, flashing me a quick smile as he drove. "Because I *was* hoping there would be a next time."

I was floating again, his words catching in my chest and bouncing around wildly, my body racing as fast as my heart.

"Then that makes two of us," I said with a smile twice as big as my face.

"But this time," he said, "I was also hoping I wouldn't have to keep using Monster GO as an excuse."

"I think we did okay without it," I said and for the first time I was reminded that my phone was still in the car's center compartment.

"Yeah, I think we survived," he agreed.

The car slowed to a stop and I realized we were suddenly back at my parents' house. I hadn't even noticed how fast the time had gone, and for a moment, I mourned that we were here. I thought about asking Jacob to drive us around the block a few times, but he was already out of the car and opening my door.

He took my hand as we walked toward the front door. My parents had left the outer light on, but the house itself was completely dark.

"I've got another date in mind," he said as we neared the door. He wrapped me in his arms and again I felt the soft silk of his shirt against my cheek.

"What's that?" I said, my words muffled as I spoke into his chest and shoulder.

"It's a surprise."

"Another one?" I asked, looking up at him in amazement.

"Another one," he said. "I didn't strike out with this one, did I?"

"Definitely not."

"Good," he said. "Then maybe I'll just keep going until I do strike out."

"Yeah, we'll see," I teased, though truthfully I wouldn't have minded. Another date with Jacob was all I wanted.

"Are you busy tomorrow?" he asked, releasing me but catching my hands as we came apart.

"Nope," I said. "You know me, just living the life of the unemployed over here."

He faked a sympathetic chuckle. "Maybe I can distract you from the pressure a little bit? If I haven't distracted you enough already."

"Oh don't worry," I assured him. "There's only so many new resumes I can send out."

"Then in that case, are we on for tomorrow?" He held his breath for a moment. I never would have noticed it if I hadn't been so close to him. He presented to the world this calm and poised persona, but it was nice to see he could be as nervous as I was about things.

"If you give me apparel instructions again," I replied. "I would have been dead in the water tonight if you didn't warn me."

"Tennis shoes and something comfortable," he said after a moment.

"Tennis shoes? We're not doing anything *athletic*, are we?" I said, winking at him.

He laughed. "I'm not thirteen anymore."

He squeezed my hands. His pulse carried through my limbs and into my chest, the epicenter of my excitement. He pulled my hands until I was close enough to kiss, and his lips landed softly on mine.

I felt him drop my hands and find his grip again on my lower back. His lips sat on mine for a while, his warmth pushing against me. His face tilted and he bit my lower lip before bringing my mouth entirely into his, our tongues dancing.

The lust in that moment was heavy and anchored me only a few feet from my front door. Part of me wanted to drag him through the door, tearing at his fancy clothes until they revealed an even better prize. But the other part of me remained anchored, not wanting the moment to end or even dissipate slightly. That and the fact that my parents were sleeping just a few rooms away.

I was attracted to him, *intensely* attracted to him, and I wanted to show it. I brought my hand behind his head and cupped his neck, pulling him into me even more. Again I felt him bite softly on my lip before releasing me right back into his kiss.

In only a few moments he had filled the night that had before seemed dark and empty. But then, as sudden and perfectly as it had started, our kiss ended, his lips lingering on mine before falling away completely.

"Will I see you tomorrow?" he whispered, his eyes still closed.

"Yes." I didn't want to open my eyes. I didn't want this moment to end.

"Goodnight," he whispered and kissed my cheek.

"Goodnight," I whispered back.

CHAPTER 8

"How long until we get there?" I asked.

I sat in the passenger seat of Jacob's car with my eyelids shut and a smile on my face. All of the nice things he had been doing for me were starting to make me feel like a princess. I loved it, but I was still a little hesitant to get my hopes up completely. With everything I was already dealing with, like trying to find work and get on my own two feet, the last thing that I needed was to get my heart broken.

"A couple of minutes," he said. "No peeking, though, okay?"

I tried to play detective and figure out what this surprise might be. He had said to dress casual, so I was wearing dark jeans with a white blouse. I'd worn comfortable shoes, even if they weren't truly tennis shoes. I really had no clue what to prepare for, though.

"Can I guess where you're taking me?" I asked. We'd transitioned from the paved road onto a dirt one, but I wasn't sure where we were yet. "Or is that not allowed?"

"You can try, but you won't be able to," he said with a chuckle.

"The old farmhouse?" It was a favorite of teens needing to get away from their parents.

"Nope," he said. "But good guess. Now just be patient for two more seconds, because we're almost there."

I sat quietly until the car pulled to a stop.

"Don't open your eyes," he reminded me.

I couldn't deny how much fun it was to have a surprise awaiting me. It almost didn't even matter what the actual surprise was either. That wasn't what made it fun. It was the anticipation, the excitement and the thought that Jacob had put into it that really made it great.

"I'll open your door for you," he said.

The engine stopped, and I listened as Jacob got out of the driver's seat. A few seconds later, he opened my door and undid my seat belt for me. He took my hand and helped me out. I wanted so badly to take a peek, but I didn't. I kept my eyes crunched together and allowed him to be my eyes as we walked away from the vehicle.

"This is so fun," I said, with a giggle.

"Just wait," he said.

We walked for a little ways. I held onto Jacob's strong arm, taking each step carefully since I couldn't see where I was going. He was patient and gave me directions and warnings about stones and things so I wouldn't trip.

"Okay, open your eyes whenever you're ready," he said as we came to a stop.

I savored the suspense for a few more seconds and then slowly pulled off the scarf and lifted my eyelids. It took less than a second before I realized where we were.

"William's Park?" I said, recognizing the familiar area.

It wasn't the park that he was surprising me with, though. It was what laid in front of us on the grass. There was a blanket spread out and on top of it, a wicker picnic basket overflowing with food. Next to the basket was a bottle of unopened champagne in a bucket of ice and two champagne flutes. He had situated the entire arrangement at the far end of the park, where there was a small opening in the bushes. On the other side was the creek that I had shown him a couple of days before, but a little bit further upstream.

"I would have set it up over in your favorite spot but I decided that I didn't want to make a mess over there," Jacob explained. "It seemed like that exact area was so special to you and I wasn't sure if you'd like a picnic anyway."

"*Like* it?" I said. "I *love* it."

I wrapped my arms around his neck and kissed him. He laughed and kissed me back, glad that I was obviously pleased.

It was just a picnic, but I couldn't have imagined a better surprise if I had tried. In fact, I almost liked it more than the expensive dinner the night before. This surprise took more thought and effort, making it feel even more romantic.

"It's perfect," I said, as I pulled away from him and looked into his eyes.

"You really like it?" he asked. "I was kind of afraid you'd think it was cheesy."

"It's not cheesy at all," I said, as I glanced back at the beautiful arrangement on the grass. "I've never had anybody do anything like this for me before. Thank you so much."

"You're welcome," he said. "I have to be honest, though. I've never had a real picnic before with anybody. I'm glad you're here to join me with it."

"Me too," I said.

We sat down on the blanket and Jacob opened the bottle of champagne.

"I've been saving this bottle for almost five years," he said, as he popped the cork. "I had always said that I'd save it for a special occasion and I figured that today was the perfect excuse."

"Is it a special occasion?" I asked, with doe eyes.

"Of course it's a special occasion," he said.

My lips curled up into an uncontrollable smile. "What do you mean?"

"Isn't a picnic in the park with a beautiful girl special occasion enough?" he asked. "I can't think of a better reason than that."

"That's the sweetest thing anybody has ever said to me," I said. "Thank you for this. Seriously, this is amazing."

Jacob's eyes lit up and he leaned toward me to give me a peck on the lips. He pulled away and looked at me, a contented expression written across his face.

"You have no idea how happy it makes me that you like this," he said. "I was seriously worried you'd think it was weird or creepy or something."

I was wearing the widest and goofiest smile I had ever had. I was dizzy with excitement. Or was it the beginning of love? I couldn't tell, since it was all happening so fast. I didn't care, though. All that mattered was that it felt amazing.

This is quickly becoming the best summer I've ever had, I thought.

Jacob sat back on the blanket and grabbed the bottle of champagne, filling up the glasses. He handed me one of them and then held his in the air. We clinked them together. "To us."

"To us," I repeated.

We both took a sip and I couldn't believe how good it was. "This is amazing. What kind of champagne is this?"

"It's Dom Perignon," he said. "My favorite."

"I don't know enough about champagne to really know what that means," I said. The bubbles tickled my nose as I took a sip. "But I can say that I think I may have found my favorite, too."

"I hope you're hungry," he said, reaching over and opening the basket. "And I also hope you don't mind that I'm not a very good cook."

I watched as he pulled out a bunch of grapes and then two sandwiches. In addition, he set out sliced cheese and crackers, some vegetables with ranch dressing and some barbecue chips. I noticed the picnic basket still had the price tag on it.

"Wow, you went all out," I said, with a smile. I pointed to the tag. "Did you buy this just for today?"

"I did." A slight blush filled his cheeks. "Remember, this is my first picnic."

How sweet is that? He went and bought a picnic basket just for this, I thought.

Jacob pulled out two paper plates and situated the food on them. He seemed so proud as he did so and it made my heart swell. I still couldn't believe that he had done all of this for me.

I leaned back and closed my eyes, enjoying all the sounds sensations around me. The summer sun dappled the ground under the trees. I could hear the creek whispering secrets to the shore as we ate. It felt like we were the only people in the entire world.

"It's so nice out," I said. "You picked the perfect day for this. It's not too cold and it's not too hot."

"It worked out," he agreed. "The perfect day with the perfect girl."

I grinned at him and popped a grape into my mouth. We sat underneath the sun, sipping our wine and eating our meal. The park was mostly empty, with just a few kids hanging out on the opposite side. They were far enough away that I could only make out their laughs as they ran around in the grass.

"I never would have imagined that Monster GO would have led me to meeting you," Jacob said, drawing my attention back to him.

"I'm as surprised as you are," I said. "I'm still in shock about it actually. I never thought I'd run into you again after that night in the restaurant. Of course, I'm sure that was clear by how messy my hair was that morning. It looked like I had just crawled out of bed. Which, admittedly, I had."

Jacob laughed as he took another sip from his champagne. "I think you looked great. I kind of like the bedhead look."

"Shush," I said, playfully pushing on his shoulder and causing him to rock back. "It really is crazy, though."

"What, your hair that morning?" he said, with a sly smile.

"No, the fact that we wouldn't have ever met again if it wasn't for that game. That's the only reason we ever came in contact. I wouldn't be sitting here right now if someone hadn't developed that app."

"Where do you think you'd be?" he asked.

I shrugged. "Probably sitting in my room and looking for jobs. Maybe I'd be at the coffee shop with Caroline. I certainly wouldn't be this happy."

He scooted across the blanket so that he was sitting right next to me, with his arm wrapped around my lower back. I leaned into him, allowing him to support my weight. It made me feel safe and loved.

"Speaking of Monster GO, how far have you gotten? How many monsters have you caught?" Jacob asked.

"Not a ton," I said. "Maybe ten or so."

"You've got to get working on that," he said. "Or Tommy will have my head."

"How many do you have?" I asked.

"You're going to think I'm the biggest dork ever, but I've only got ten left to catch," he said.

"Aren't there like two-hundred and fifty of them total?" I asked, a little impressed.

"There are actually only one hundred and five. Not only do I have most of them, I also have duplicates of almost all of the ones that I *do* have," he said.

"Can I have some of them?" I asked.

"I'd love to give you some, but it doesn't work that way," he explained. He paused and looked at me carefully. "You'd really want to trade them?"

"Why not? Wouldn't it be better if there was a function in the game where you could trade Monsters? Think about it. If I happened to have one you didn't have, you'd happily trade one of your duplicates for it."

"A trading function, huh?" Jacob said, his eyes going distant as he thought about it. "Sounds interesting."

"I'm just saying. I think it would make a whole lot of sense," I replied. My mind was already figuring out how to code for something like that. "It would make the game more playable for all players and it wouldn't be that hard to code for."

"That's actually a really good idea," Jacob said. "I can't believe they haven't thought of that yet."

"I'm telling you, I should try to find a job where all I do is sit around and think of ideas for these games all day," I said.

"You'd be good at it," he said, before kissing me on the cheek. "You've got that creative edge that a lot of program-mers don't have. It seems like you see the big picture of a program and not just all of the lines of code that go into creating it."

"Honestly, the creative side of it is my favorite part. I like the coding, too. In fact, I was top of my class in nearly every programming course in college." I paused, not wanting to brag. "But I'm just not passionate about it the way that I am with the creative element. That's what makes me excited."

"Why don't you find a job that allows you to be more creative then?" he asked. "I know that they're out there, especially with all of the apps and games that are created every day."

"I've seen a few openings, but I'm under-qualified for all of them. They all want someone who has years and years of experience, and experience is something that I don't have. All I've got is ingenuity and blind ambition."

"Sometimes that's all you need, though," he said.

"I suppose," I said. "But I still haven't been able to make it work for me. Any ingenuity I have is being wasted on updating my resume ten times a day. It doesn't leave much time for creating anything at all, except eye strain from staring at job openings online."

"Alicia, it's only been a couple of weeks, right?" he asked.

"Yeah." I plucked a blade of grass and twirled it between my fingers.

"Well, give it a little more time. Try to be patient. Trust me, a job will come. And when it does, you'll look back and realize that all of this worry you're having was in vain." He smiled at me. "At some point, you might even wish that you were jobless again, sitting with me in the park and drinking wine in the middle of the day."

"You're probably right." I tossed the blade of grass away. "The grass is always greener on the other side."

"Always." Jacob agreed. "What other ideas do you have for the game?"

"You really want to know?" I tipped back the last swig of champagne and then set the glass next to me on the blanket. My belly was full of good food and good drink.

"I do," he assured me. "I'm interested in your thoughts."

I grinned at him. Jacob laid back on the blanket and I crawled up next to him, placing my head onto his chest. I listened to his heartbeat and his breathing. I knew that the rhythmic sound would eventually pull me into sleep if I let it.

"I think there should be player battles. Not just at gyms, but against other players individually," I began. "Then, if you do that, there should also be a friend's list so you can see if your friends are nearby or even other people who are interested in playing."

I grinned, excited as ideas came to me. "Also, custom tracking items, gym notifications, friend notifications, custom lures-"

"Whoa, hold on there." Jacob held up his hands. "I had no idea you had so many ideas. Some of those are really good."

"Thanks. The friends stuff wouldn't be hard since it could be tied into the log-in information," I said with a smile. I winced in embarrassment as I realized I had gone a little overboard. "But, now I'm going computer geek on you and that's not really part of our date."

"But, it is a part of who you are," Jacob replied gently. "So I like it. Keep talking. I'll take notes."

I laughed as he pulled out his phone and pretended to write stuff down. I started telling him just how I would implement each option. The friends list would be imported from social media, the lures could be purchased or earned. I even started telling him how I would code for it.

He kept up with me, asking me questions and making my ideas even better. It was just too bad that no one from Monster GO was there to hear our brainstorming session, because it would have made them millions of dollars.

We were discussing how to do alerts when both of our phones vibrated.

"Must be a Monster nearby," he said, switching on the application. I shook my head at him, but pulled out my phone as well.

As soon as I looked at the screen, I nearly dropped my phone in surprise. A Legazeus was nearby. Normally, this wouldn't have meant a single thing to me. But Tommy had been talking about this particular Monster for weeks now, pretty much since the game came out.

He said the Legazeus was one of the rarest Monsters. They only ever showed up in special places, and nobody ever knew when or where that will be. I remembered him saying that the last one to appear was in Central Park and caused a major traffic jam due to people stopping to catch it.

"These are rare, right?" I asked, not believing what I was seeing on the screen.

"Insanely rare," he said. He grinned at me. "Let's catch it."

We held up our phones and lined the camera up with the cartoon looking character. It looked like a Centaur. It jumped around on the screen as I attempted to catch it with the Monster Catcher.

I missed on the first try and I got nervous. I knew it was only a game, but this thing was rare and I didn't want to see it go before I could add it to my inventory. Tommy would freak out if he saw that I had one, and that was where the majority of my motivation came from.

With a swipe on my screen, I tossed another Monster Catcher toward the Monster and it landed a few feet away from it.

"Darn it," I said, my body filling with anxiety.

"Don't overthink it," Jacob coached. "Just pretend it's a Fireliz."

I drew in a deep breath and slowly exhaled. With my nerves calmed, I attempted one last catch. I swiped my screen and watched the Monster Catcher fly up into an arch above the Legazeus. My breathing stopped as it began to fall.

Come on. Don't miss, I thought.

Relief filled me as the Monster Catcher landed directly on top of the creature, capturing it and adding it to my inventory.

"Thank God," I whispered. "Did you catch it, too?"

"Not yet," he said, as he brought his focus to his own phone. He had been helping me catch mine so he hadn't had a chance yet. Like a professional, though, he tossed one Monster Catcher toward the Legazeus and caught it immediately. "Got it."

"You're too good at this," I said, shaking my head.

Jacob smiled and parted his lips to respond, but before he could, a group of young boys came running up. They walked right across our blanket, shouting in excitement.

"Oh, my God," one said. "It really *is* a Legazeus. I can't believe this."

There were five of them and they all looked to be about the same age as Tommy.

"This is insane," another said. "We've got to tell Alan about this. He's going to freak."

Jacob and I looked at each other and chuckled. It wasn't too surprising that they had run over for such a rare Monster, but it was amazing at how little they cared that they were practically standing on our picnic.

Not more than thirty seconds passed before a mother and her two kids came up. They all had their phones out, including the mom.

"This can't be happening," the mom said. "Barbara is never going to believe this."

She smiled at me, with a look in her eyes that was more enthusiastic than her kids. The parents were just as into this game as the kids.

The original five boys caught the Monster and after a few tries, so did the Mom and her kids. Jacob and I took a breath as they walked away.

"That was interesting," I said. "I didn't expect that."

"Neither did I," he said. "Man, they came out of nowhere, didn't they?"

There was hustle and bustle behind us, coming from the direction of the parking lot. I turned around to see a line of cars pulling up. The parking spots became filled in seconds and people spilled out, all running toward us with their cell phones out. There were folks of all ages making their way toward our private picnic area.

"Jacob, what's happening?" I asked.

"That latest update, the one that expanded the map and put street names on," he said. "It must be bringing people from all over. They saw the Legazeus and they're coming to catch it."

Things started to look like a movie. Everyone moved like a swarm of zombies, walking quickly across the park, making their way toward us. Their arms were held out like zombies, too. The only difference is that they held cell phones in their hands. It was insane. But what had me even more shocked than their erratic and excitable behavior was the sheer number of them. Hundreds. Literally hundreds of people swarmed the park, all within a matter of minutes.

"Jacob, we should go," I said. There were more people showing up every minute, and all of them were headed straight for our picnic site. I wasn't sure we were going to be able to get out of the park.

"I agree," he said. He looked a little despondent.

We stood up from the blanket and quickly rolled everything up in it, stuffing it into the picnic basket. Before we could even finish, though, we became completely surrounded by people. They were all shouting in excitement about the Legazeus. Every single one of them was there for the same reason, and they were all rushing, knowing that this particular Monster wouldn't be there for very long.

Jacob looked upset as he bundled up the picnic things and pushed through the crowd.

"Is everything okay?" I asked. I had to practically shout to make sure I was heard over everybody.

"Yeah, I just wanted this to be special and it feels like it's ruined." When we got to the car, he threw everything in the trunk and then opened the passenger door for me. "It's kind of cool to witness this kind of craziness from a game, but I wish it hadn't ruined our picnic. This wasn't at all how I planned it. I should have thought about this a little more."

I laughed and squeezed his arm. "Jacob, it didn't ruin anything and there is no way you could have predicted that a Legazeus would show up."

"If you say so," he mumbled.

"I mean our picnic is obviously done now, but think about how memorable this is. We'll never forget this moment, as long as we live," I said, as I pointed back toward where we had been seated. There was a swarm of people, and where there had once been a picnic, now looked more like a mosh pit at a concert.

"I guess you're right," he reluctantly said. "I just had no idea there were even this many people playing the game here. The town isn't exactly a Monster GO hotspot."

Overhead, a helicopter whirred. I had no idea how this many people had found this spot so fast.

I squealed in excitement. "I'm so excited to show Tommy. He's going to flip out when he sees it. This Monster is all he's talked about since the game came out."

Jacob walked around to the driver's side and hopped in. He started up the car and began to back up, before realizing there was no way we'd be leaving any time too soon. People and cars had congested the parking lot and the road out of the park.

"How long until the Legazeus disappears?" I asked as Jacob turned off the engine.

"The rare ones won't last more than twenty minutes," he said. "I guess we'll have to wait for a little bit."

I shook my head in awe as I looked through the windshield. In just the few seconds that it had taken Jacob and I to get to his car, the horde had grown substantially in size.

"At least we have something to watch," I commented as yet more people streamed past our car. The helicopter was making another loop over the park and I had a feeling this would be on the evening news.

"How are this many people here?" Jacob asked, annoyance in his voice. "These kinds of crowds are exactly the reason I moved away from the Valley."

"You don't like crowds?" I asked, looking over at him.

Jacob put on his dark sunglasses and pulled a baseball

cap out from under his seat. He shook his head. "I hate crowds. Especially crowds having to do with the game."

The phrasing seemed funny, but I just shrugged. "I'm sorry. We'll be out of here soon. Do you want me to drive?"

"No, I'm fine to drive." He sighed and did an attempt at a smile. "I just wasn't expecting this. I wanted a fun, memorable afternoon with you. Not a zoo."

"Totally not your fault," I reminded him.

"If you say so," he replied. He hunkered down in his seat and pulled down the brim of his cap. "Only ten more minutes before it disappears."

I shook my head, and looked down at my phone. I had caught a monster that most people would never even see in the game. It made me think of my trading idea and for a moment I wished I had the ear of the game designer. It would be so much fun to play the game with him.

CHAPTER 9

*A*fter almost forty minutes, Jacob and I were finally able to get out of the craziness in the park. Luckily, Jacob had a tablet in his car, so we used the time to continue creating the imaginary updates for the game.

I couldn't believe what the game was capable of. I hadn't experienced anything like it in my life. One minute, we were enjoying a peaceful picnic and the next we were practically getting trampled over by a bunch of tweens and their parents, all in an effort to catch a rare Monster. I was still excited to tell Tommy about what had happened, but that was going to have to wait until I got back home. My date wasn't over yet.

"Thanks for agreeing to finish our date at my place," Jacob said, as he pulled off of the highway. "I had no idea that was going to happen."

"How could you? That was crazy," I said, as I reached over from the passenger seat and touched his arm. "I didn't want the date to be cut short either, so this works out perfectly."

"I still can't believe what happened back there," he said.

"I know the game is popular, but I never expected that. Especially not here."

"No kidding," I said. "Did you see how many parents that were there, too? They seemed just as excited as the kids."

"Pretty amazing," he agreed. "I'm just glad we got out of there before we got trampled."

I couldn't help but to laugh. "That would have been kind of a lame way to die. I can picture the headlines now. *Couple Trampled In Search of Rare Monster*."

Jacob chuckled. "That wouldn't be cool at all. If we died like that, I'd hope that someone would at least make a better story out of it. Like maybe we jumped in to save a kid from the crowd and we ended up getting trampled ourselves."

"That does sound a lot better than dying for a phone game," I agreed.

We drove for another five minutes before Jacob turned into an apartment complex near the edge of town. It was a nice area, one that I didn't frequent often because I never knew anyone who lived there. It was usually referred to as the 'rich side of town.' This apartment complex seemed to fit right in.

"You live here? At The Boulevard?" I asked. The apartments looked even nicer up close than they did from the highway.

"Yep." He shrugged. "I pretty much looked up apartments online and this place had the best reviews so I went with it."

I couldn't imagine what he was spending for rent at the place. Even the crummy little apartments on the other side of town were renting for almost double what I paid for my college apartment. Housing was scarce in our town, so prices were high.

"They look really nice from out here," I said, admiring the floor to ceiling windows that adorned the apartments.

Jacob pulled his SUV around to the back and into a multi-leveled parking garage. We drove all the way up to the top, where he parked. "You ready?"

Jacob opened the trunk and gathered the picnic basket, blanket and bottle of wine; all of the things that we'd stuffed in the car during our escape from the park. I hopped out and looked around.

Every car in here is super nice, I thought.

Lexus, BMW, Audi, and even a couple of Tesla models filled the garage. It made me feel like I was at a car show. Jacob walked stepped around the back of his SUV and took my hand.

"This way," he said, with a fake British accent that caused me to giggle. Now that we were away from the Monster GO crowd, his confidence and positive attitude had come back.

I followed Jacob into the hallway the led to his apartment. He unlocked the door and held it open for me. When I stepped inside, my eyes went straight to the very back where the floor to ceiling windows were. The view overlooked a lake and I could even see the park where we had first met.

"Is that the fountain?" I asked.

"Yes, it is," he said, glancing over at the window as he set his sunglasses and hat on the kitchen counter. "It's actually the view that made me go to the park that day. It just looked like people were having fun and it was too beautiful not to go look."

I said a silent thank you to the window for providing Jacob the impetus to go out. Sticking out of the park was the giant white fountain where Tommy had led me that first day to play Monster GO. It was a ways away, but I could still see tiny figures of people standing around it.

"I'll bet Tommy is there," I said, with a smile. I went over to the balcony door and held it open so Jacob could carry our picnic outside.

"It wouldn't surprise me," Jacob said. "Thanks for holding the door."

"My pleasure," I replied with a grin as he walked past.

"There we go," he said as he settled the basket onto the corner of the blanket he'd just rolled out. "We've got a view of the park and the sun is still out. It's basically as good of a picnic as any."

"I love it," I said. "Do you mind if I use your restroom real quick? I just want to wash my hands before we have our second picnic."

Jacob smiled and then motioned toward the upper part of his place. "The bathroom is at the top of the stairs to the right. Can't miss it."

I turned and made my way toward the stairs. I glanced around, surprised at how spacious his apartment was. Vaulted ceilings, a gigantic living room with an even bigger TV, and a beautiful dining set were the first things I noticed. There were still unopened packing boxes everywhere, stacked on the kitchen counter and the floor in nearly every corner. It was clear that Jacob had quite a bit of work to do in order to get unpacked.

This place is so nice, I thought. *It makes the place that Caroline and I lived in during college look like an actual rat's nest.*

The image of our tiny college apartment flashed into my mind. The thought of the brown carpet and nicotine-stained walls from the college kids before us made me cringe.

Once I got to the top of the stairs, I looked to my left. The master bedroom was there and Jacob's giant bed was in the center. There were windows filling that room as well. He had the same amazing view from his bed as he did from his balcony. It took a little effort to stop myself from being nosy. Instead, I just turned around and quickly washed my hands and fixed my hair in the nearby bathroom before returning downstairs.

By the time I got back to the patio, Jacob had completely rebuilt the picnic. The blanket was laid out and the picnic basket was in the center again. On each side was a full glass of the amazing red wine, which he had perfect poured in my absence.

"This is great, Jacob," I said, stepping out onto the patio to join him. "Honestly, I think I like this more than when it was at the park."

"The best part about my patio is that no matter what, we won't get trampled over by a bunch of soccer moms," he said with a wink.

I took a seat next to him on the blanket and snuggled close. He wrapped his arm around me and handed me my glass of wine.

"Cheers," I said, clinking my glass against his.

We sipped our wine and Jacob moved his hand gently up and down my lower back. I looked toward him, admiring the way the sunlight blanketed his face. He smiled when he caught me looking.

"You're cute," I said.

He leaned in and kissed my cheek. "No, you're the one who's cute."

I caught his face in my hands, and then angled in to kiss him. I had meant it to be a fairly quick kiss, something playful yet more than a peck on the check. But, when he kissed me, it quickly turned into something else.

Heat coursed down my spine, sending tingles of desire

through my nerves. Jacob felt it too. He kissed me harder, pulling me into him with his hands and his mouth. I went from simply wanting a kiss to wanting so, so much more.

Panting, I sat back and pulled my hair from my face. I didn't want to be too forward, especially not since the other day where he had turned me down. If he wanted to keep going slow, I could do slow. It was respectful and honorable.

I liked that, but I was ready for a little speed. *Respectful* and *honorable* were overrated.

Moving slowly, I brought my hand to his arm and crawled into his lap so that I was straddling him.

I pressed my chest out a little, wanting him to notice. When I did, his eyes moved down my front and then back to my face. His pupils dilated slightly, despite the fact that they were almost in direct sunlight.

He brought his mouth to mine, filling me with the taste of his lips. There was passion behind the kiss that made me heating. There was no way I was going to be able to back off again if he kept this up. I wanted him.

In between my legs and underneath the front of Jacob's slacks, I felt something that hadn't been there when I had first straddled him. His cock was already firm and pressing against me. I could feel it through my jeans. It was the sexiest thing to know that he wanted me as bad as I wanted him.

I kissed him again, and this time I found myself grinding down on the bulge. Jacob let out a guttural moan as I guided my body upward along his length. When I broke the kiss, I notice that the expression on his face had changed. He looked at me with wild eyes and licked his lips. No words needed to be exchanged. We both knew what we were feeling. It was an unspoken thing. We wanted each other and clearly we were going to take what we wanted. We were done waiting.

Jacob's hands drifted down my thighs and landed on my rear. He pulled me upward, sliding me along his length once again. My body tingled with delight and heat started to surge .

"Upstairs?" he asked.

I nodded, unable to speak coherently.

I wasn't sure what in the heck had gotten into me. For the most part, I was a pretty shy girl. I'd have imagined that some boys would have even called me a prude, at least during the dates where I didn't have sex. But Jacob was different. He had treated me like a princess in every encounter I had ever had with him.

The connection we had was more than just sexual. I knew he was going to treat me right afterwards. I knew this wasn't going to be a one-night stand. This was just the beginning of a wonderful relationship. I felt safe with him.

He sat up, and we crawled to our feet. Jacob placed on arm at my lower back and the other behind me knees, and then he lifted me from the ground in one swift movement. I giggled as I wrapped my arm around his neck to hang on for the ride.

Jacob stepped through the patio doors to make our way back into his apartment and I almost commented on it. I felt like saying something about how this must be what it feels like to get married and carried over the threshold. I bit my tongue, though, fearing that a comment like that could easily ruin the moment.

As he carried me across the living room, I playfully nibbled on his ear and neck. I breathed him in, too, letting his scent make its way into my nose. His musk, his stubble, his strength; it all had me going crazy.

Once at the top of the stairs, we went straight to his bedroom. My lips still tingled from our kiss, but it wasn't enough to satiate the desperate craving that I had going on inside of me. We approached the bed and he set me down so that I was standing on the floor next to him.

"You're so beautiful," he whispered reverently. His eyes moved up and down my body, giving me an obvious once over.

Not even a second passed before we resumed our kiss. This time, there was more passion behind it than ever. Something about being in his bedroom, and what that insinuated, caused both of us to let go. Our walls dropped and with it, our lust for each other flooded out, raging through us.

A soft moan crept into my throat as our lips pressed together. My hands drifted up and down his front, feeling his chest and abs under my fingertips. There was only a thin layer of clothing between us, and I wanted it removed. I was done waiting. So without breaking our kiss, I unbuttoned the top few buttons of his shirt and placed my hands onto his pectorals.

The smell of his cologne continued to fill my nostrils and I breathed deeper, letting his scent soak into my senses. Without even realizing it, I had wrapped one of my legs behind his. I had pulled myself as close to him as possible. I couldn't get enough. I had become greedy for his touch. I only wanted more.

I broke the kiss just long enough to look him in the eyes.

"Take me." The words dripped off of my tongue without going through my mind's filter. I didn't care, though. It was exactly what I wanted and in that moment, I was certainly not afraid to say it.

Jacob grunted in reply, a primal sound that perfectly fit

the desire in his eyes. He just took a step closer, causing my butt to collide with the edge of the mattress. I laid back, falling into his soft comforter. Jacob crawled over me immediately, and brought his lips to the outside of my neck.

"Oh, God," I whispered.

He nibbled the sensitive skin, sending chills of pleasure through my body. He bit just hard enough to invoke a little pain, but then would pull away and hit the same spot with a sensual kiss. It had me trembling below him, wanting more by the second.

Jacob let out a sexual growl as he moved his face down my chest. He kissed the top of my cleavage as he undid the buttons of my blouse. I arched my back and pressed my tits toward his face, urging him on.

He kissed between them, as he continued to unbutton my shirt all the way to the bottom. When he opened it up, my bra was revealed. Normally, I'd have felt a little shy. I didn't have the biggest or most amazing breasts, but Jacob made me feel sexy and confident in a way that no other man had. So without any hesitation, I unclasped my bra, releasing my chest to him.

"Alicia... you're..." Jacob whispered, as he admired my front. "...So beautiful."

Leaning forward, he closed his mouth over my right nipple. I let out a low moan as he bombarded the sensitive nub with his tongue. A wave of pleasure pumped through me and the desperation growing between my legs began to throb. He licked circles around the nipple and clamped his lips over it before drawing away, creating a wet kissing noise.

Immediately, he brought his face to the other breast and gave it equal attention. He was slow and attentive as he pleasured me. It seemed like each movement of his tongue was thought out and precise, with no other purpose in the world except to fill me with sensation.

After a minute, he pushed himself up and looked me over. He eyed me with an expression of desperate lust. The beautiful blue-color of his eyes were now mostly black, dilated with adrenaline.

The bulge underneath the front of his slacks had grown. As he undid his belt, he shot me a confident and sexy-as-hell smile. My mouth watered, anticipating what was underneath that clothing. I wanted it. I wanted every inch of him.

Jacob pulled the belt off of the pants and tossed it across the room. Then he undid the button and zipper, before sliding them down. He was fully erect under his boxers and the head of his cock pressed out against the thin material.

He paused, cocking his head and raising one eyebrow. I licked my lips and nodded. His confident smirk widened as he undid his shirt the rest of the way and let it drop to the floor at his feet.

He crawled back over me, bringing his hands to my breasts before kissing me once more. I wrapped my legs around his waist and pulled him closer. I could feel his hardness against me, even through my jeans. He was so firm and so turned on. It made me want him even more.

My body craved him, and I didn't want any more foreplay. I wanted him inside of me right then. No more flirtation, no more games.

I reached down and undid the button on my jeans. Jacob slipped his finger into the waist and tugged downward. I lifted my butt from the bed to aid him in removing the pants. With a couple of gentle yet powerful jerks on the clothing, Jacob had me laying there in only my panties.

He looked me over, and the expression of lust in his face became even more apparent. He clenched his jaw and swallowed, his eyes moving up and down my body, before resting on my panties. I slipped my thumbs into the waist strap of my underwear and began to pull them down. But before I could, Jacob grabbed them and slid them all the way down my legs.

"I want you so bad," he said, his voice gruff and his words trailing off at the end.

My underwear was loosely hanging around my ankles and I kicked them off, watching them soar to the opposite side of the room. They landed on the top of his dresser, right next to a bottle of his cologne.

Jacob stood in front of me. He was glorious in his nakedness. I laid there for a moment, just admiring the way he looked. I loved the way his chest and abs moved with his breathing. His hair was a little messy, too, which somehow made him look even sexier. In this moment, he seemed untamed and wild. The clean cut Jacob that most people probably knew was nowhere to be found in this room. He had left that Jacob in an office somewhere. The man that was currently in front of me was instinctual and masculine, exactly what I wanted.

I teased him with my feet, dragging my toes over the front of his naked thighs. It was my way of beckoning him back toward me. He didn't do exactly as I had expected, though. Instead, he draped one of my legs over each of his shoulders and then dropped to his knees. His face was now between my thighs and his beard stubble tickled my sensitive skin as he inched toward my pleasure center.

Jacob kissed the crease between my thigh and my flower. His lips touched down ever so gently, before pulling away and moving to the other side. I trembled, awaiting his touch, wanting him to just give me that tongue in the right spot.

He teased me until I couldn't take it anymore. Using my legs, I pulled him closer.

"Stop teasing me. Please, just do it," I begged.

Finally, he let out a soft growl and faced forward, lapping his tongue against my sex. I grabbed a handful of his hair and pulled his mouth toward me, squealing as pleasure took the place of the aching desire.

"Yes..." I groaned, so quietly that the sound barely made it to the outside of my lips.

He flicked his tongue against the top of my pussy, bombarding it in the same way as he had my nipples. It caused a chill of ecstasy to course through every inch of my body.

"Just like that," I whispered, as Jacob focused his attention on my clit.

Jacob let out a soft groan and the vibration from it made the pleasure even more intense. I squeezed my thighs, pressing his head between them like a vice. My back arched and my breasts rose in the air. I began bucking my hips upward toward his mouth, wanting him to taste me deeper, wishing I could make the friction between us even more intense.

He placed his hands onto the top of my thighs and spread my legs out a few inches. Then he began moving his tongue downward, pleasuring the length of my lips, before coming back up to dance around my clit once again. He did this over and over, causing my body to fill to the brim with sensation.

"I'm coming," I gasped, barely able to whisper the words before pleasure took over my senses.

He lapped his tongue even more quickly against me. It sent me over the top. I couldn't hold back any more. The dam had broken and the ecstasy that pumped into my body overcame my ability to slow it down. I let out a squeal that filled the apartment as I climaxed, squeezing my thighs over his head once more. The world dissolved around me and my body trembled as I gripped my hands into fists through Jacob's hair. I rode out the orgasm until the pleasure finally tapered off. As soon as it faded, I relaxed into the bed. A contented smile was plastered across my face.

Breathe, Alicia. Breathe, I thought, reminding myself that oxygen was still an important element to survival. Though, right at that moment, I certainly didn't feel like I needed it.

I drew in a long breath and finally released my grip from his hair. I also relaxed my thighs so that he could pull his head away for the first time since he had dropped to his knees. When he stood up, he seemed even more eager than before and his dick showed it as well. It was twitching now, throbbing in rhythm to his increased heart rate.

Never in my life had I wanted someone so badly. I physically *needed* him in that moment. He must have seen it in my eyes, because he didn't hesitate to step close. He lifted my legs and pressed them toward my chest. The head of his cock hovered just outside of my opening, so close that I could feel the heat as it radiated off of it. He held there for a second. I could see that he wanted to plunge in, but there was a moment of hesitation.

"Do you want me to use a condom?" he asked.

I wanted to feel *him,* not rubber. Plus, I was on birth control anyway and I trusted him. So I didn't even respond to his question. Instead, I bit my bottom lip as I dropped my legs and wrapped them around his waist. Then I pulled him toward me.

His crown pressed into my flower and we both let out a deep groan. I closed my eyes and leaned my head back.

Jacob bucked his hips forward, sliding further into me. I exploded with wetness, coating his length as he entered.

My body trembled on the bed as Jacob slid all the way in. Our bodies were now entwined and the desperate throbbing that had been persuading me to make love to him had been replaced with a deep and content pleasure.

Jacob held himself over me and began to rock his hips forward and back. His pace was slow at first. It seemed like he was savoring the sensation of being inside of me.

"That feels so good," I whispered, my words wavering.

He grunted softly in response and then quickened his pace. Each thrust caused a surge of bliss to pump into me, deeper and deeper each time. I began to squeal out in pleasure. I couldn't help it. It was just too much sensation to hold back.

I dropped my hands and gripped the comforter below me. Jacob clenched his jaw. Then he began to pound into me. His body slammed against mine, and each time he entered me, a jolt of pleasure followed. My body overflowed with ecstasy and it poured out of my skin, electrifying the air surrounding us. Every cell in my body drowned in pleasure and breathing became something that I had to remind myself to do.

"Yes, just like that," I said, though I wasn't sure if the words even made it out of my throat.

Jacob kept pace and I felt myself rising toward orgasm for the second time that day. When it happened, I couldn't even make a sound. I held my breath and closed my eyes, letting the feeling envelope me. My entire body clamped down around him as I rode the wave all the way up, becoming lost in the dizzying bliss.

I gripped the comforter hard, feeling the material slide between my fingers, as the final swell of pleasure washed over me. When it passed, I opened my eyes and released my grip from the blanket. My hands were trembling now, and so were my legs. My entire body stammered on the bed beneath Jacob.

Jacob's skin was now covered in a light layer of sweat, accentuating the lines between his muscles. I watched as his face began to contort and his cheeks turned red. The pace of his thrusts increased and he let out an animalistic grunt.

I knew what was coming. I nodded quickly, ready to take all of him inside of me. I watched as he held his breath and closed his eyes. The room was silent, but just for a fleeting instant.

"Yes," he grunted, his voice the only sound in the apartment.

He broke apart within me, losing the control. It was the sexiest thing I had ever seen to watch him come apart, because of me- inside of me. He was always so careful, so in control, that to see him break at the seams was enough to nearly send me over the edge a third time.

Finally, he breathed again and opened his eyes. He wore a dazed, yet content, expression on his face. He stayed inside of me and leaned forward to give me a sensual kiss. Our skin was slick with sweat and our fingers grazed smoothly over each other's bodies as we lay entangled on his bed.

"That was amazing," I whispered, breaking our kiss.

Jacob nodded in agreement. "You're incredible."

He crawled up next to me on the bed and wrapped an arm over my belly, holding me close. He kissed my cheek and the top of my shoulder in a sweet way that made me smile. It made me feel safe and loved.

That was by far the best sex I've ever had, I thought. *Is there anything about Jacob that isn't flawless?*

The question instantly caused a twinge of doubt to creep into my mind.

This man is everything that I could ever want. What's "the catch"? There's always a catch. He's too perfect, I thought. *If something is too good to be true, then it probably is, right?*

I pushed the thought away. We had just shared something special and I wasn't about to let my wandering thoughts ruin this moment for me. I was happy. I was content and I wasn't going to start worrying about things that I had no control over.

We laid there quietly on his bed. Despite the fact that my mind was churning, it still only took a few seconds for me to close my eyes, letting the sound of Jacob's breathing lull me to sleep.

CHAPTER 10

The next morning, I sat at a table in the corner of the coffee shop while I waited for Caroline. Since I was on the opposite side of town, I'd called her only a few moments after getting home from Jacob's apartment demanding we meet up soon. And she'd agreed without any hesitation.

Besides, I knew she liked coffee shops and I knew she liked double shot espressos with caramel and almond milk. I'd already ordered her one and a vanilla mocha for myself. Her drink sat across the table and right in front of her chair in what I hoped would be an enticing sight, something like using a bone to call a dog. If nothing else I wanted to bring her mood to a level near mine, and for Caroline, coffee was always the answer.

The coffee shop was bustling at nine-thirty in the morning and I appreciated being able to sit and wait contentedly. It was the beginning of a warm day without any fog that sometimes accompanied California mornings.

Even the sun is in a good mood, I thought.

Caroline wore a tight red skirt and a black t-shirt. She

didn't take off her sunglasses until she'd found me sitting at the table. She dropped her purse on the table and removed her wallet before realizing that I'd already bought her drink.

"Double shot espresso with caramel and milk?" she asked.

"Yep," I said.

"Almond milk?" She raised an eyebrow.

"Yep," I said again. I nudged her drink a little closer.

"You're the best." She used the straw to stir her drink as she grinned at me.

"And I told them to go light on the ice," I said, feeling rather proud of myself.

"Wow, I was wondering if they'd finally caught on, but look at you." She grinned and took a sip. "You must have good news."

I beamed back with something between a smile and long smirk. "Maybe."

She sipped at her drink after taking a seat in the chair across from me. "Are you going to make me beg?"

I allowed my smile to grow even more, drawing out the moment as well as my excitement.

"Fine," she said. "I'll let you sit with your hysteria for a sec. I'm actually going to go grab a breakfast burrito or something. You want anything?"

"I'm good," I said, still smiling.

I watched Caroline order her burrito. She glanced over at me and narrowed her eyes and I knew she was mad I still had my secret. It wasn't often that I had anything good like this, so I was enjoying keeping her waiting. She returned with a burrito in hand, blowing on it viciously.

"You ready to talk?" she said, beating her fist against the table in a jokingly dramatic manor.

"Is this an interrogation now?" I asked. "I need to know if I need my lawyer."

"You might," she threatened. "Unless you're ready to spill the beans?"

"Oh I'm ready," I said, allowing my same smile to engross my face again. "It's about Jacob..."

"I assumed." She rolled her eyes playfully at me.

"Are you going to *let* me spill the beans or are you going to interrupt?" I said, my giddy mood turning into a motivation to play with Caroline a little more.

"You're ridiculous," she replied. "I'm starting to think this was all a ploy."

"Oh, it's very real. But be patient, I've gotta start from the beginning." I cleared my throat as Caroline watched me speak with inquiring eyes.

"*Anyway*," I continued, "Jacob said he wanted to take me on a picnic, totally his idea. He brought everything. The picnic basket, the blanket, the food- all of it. He got us all set up in William's Park."

"Wait, William's Park? There was a Legazues there," Caroline said. Her eyes went wide. "Did you get one?"

"I did, but that's not the important part of my story." I couldn't stop the grin spreading over my face. "We had to leave after it showed up since the park was packed, but, then we went back to his place."

I grinned way too wide and Caroline's eyes went wide as she figured out the rest of my story. All of Caroline's anticipation finally made its way to the surface and blossomed into an eruption of delighted whoops. It was the moment I'd been waiting for.

I looked around to see if her outburst had caused the surrounding tables to stare. Luckily, no one was looking at us.

"Way. To. Go," she said slowly and emphatically. "So how was he?"

"He was wonderful," I said. "He's excellent. Amazing. Spectacular."

"His eyes still the best part?" she joked.

"He has *many* best parts," I said. "Basically the last forty-eight hours have been incredible. A dinner date, a half-picnic date and then going back to his place. I'm living in a happy dream right now."

"What was his place like?" Caroline played with her straw, drinking in her coffee and all my details.

"He lives at The Boulevard, so it was really fancy," I said. "He's still moving in, so it was mostly just boxes."

"That's nice." She grinned at me and got straight to the topic she wanted to discuss. "So, when do I get to meet him?" she asked, her signature smile curling at the edge of her mouth.

"Soon," I said. "I'm still getting to know him myself."

"Oh come on," she said, setting her coffee down. "I'm sure you've met some of his friends."

"I haven't, actually." It wasn't until I said it that I even realized that I hadn't even heard him mention any of his friends. It was probably just due to him having just moved here.

"Then I can get the ball rolling," she said, her smile turning into an enthusiastic grin of delight. "We'll have a barbecue. Or better yet, a party."

"Slow down." I held my hand up like it was a stop sign. Not that it would slow her down any. "I'm not about to bombard him and freak him out."

"With your freak of a friend?" She raised her eyebrows at me.

"Not my *freak* friend, my best friend," I said, waving her

off. "But I just kind of want to take things slow and let them play out. I think I might've really found something good here and I don't want to scare him off. He's not big on crowds, so a party probably wouldn't be his thing."

"I guess that's fine." Caroline let out a dramatic sigh. "But, I claim dibs on meeting him next."

"Deal." I grinned at her. "I'm just so excited about him. I think I can see a future with him, but I might just be fooling myself."

"Can you see him opening presents on Christmas?" Caroline asked, her face unreadable. I wasn't sure where she was going with this question.

I thought for a moment. He would probably start out opening them carefully, but end up ripping the wrapping paper as soon as he got excited. I could already see him in my minds' eye: the two of us in pajamas at my parents' house with cups of coffee and Tommy running around like a maniac. The image made me smile.

"Yeah, I can."

"I'm assuming that dopey grin on your face is because you're there too," Caroline said, drawing me back to the present. "You see yourself with him."

"I do," I replied with a nod. "What is the point of your question?"

"You see yourself with him in six months," Caroline explained. "I'm guessing that you can see a bunch of other holidays with him, too."

"I guess I do." I sat there for a moment, realizing that Caroline was right. I saw a future with Jacob. A real future. Not just little snippets or things that might happen, but actual events. I wanted to have him share my family at Christmas. I wanted to visit his parents for the Thanksgiving. I wanted to share my life with him.

"Then you see a future with him," she informed me. "I can't wait to meet this guy."

She wasn't going to give up on meeting him, so I changed the subject.

"Any good news on your end?" I asked, innocently sipping at my coffee. "You know, any teacher news or anything?"

"No," she replied. She narrowed her eyes, knowing exactly what I was doing, but she let me get away with changing topics anyway. "Nothing yet. It's pretty saturated teaching wise around here. I'm starting to think I might have to expand my hunting grounds."

"Not a bad idea," I agreed. "I've started sending applications as far west as Denver."

"I haven't gone quite that far," she said. "But I might have to start looking in LA or something. Maybe even San Francisco."

"I'd come visit you all the time if you moved there." I sighed and shrugged. "Time to go chase careers like real adults."

"What about you?" Caroline asked. She slurped the last little bit of coffee up through her straw. "Any job offers?"

"Nothing," I said with a sad shake of my head. "Unless you want to count a prestigious part-time offer from Dairy King."

She shook her head. "How is it you managed to land the perfect guy, but can't get a job?"

"I have no idea," I replied. "I just wish I had half as much luck on the job on front as I did on the dating one."

"Me too," she agreed. Her phone vibrated and she swiped at the screen before holding it up to show the monster nearby notification. "But, at least we'll always have

Monster GO, and if we have that, then who needs dating and jobs?"

THE HOUSE WAS silent when I arrived home. Dad was at work, and Mom had left a note that she and Tommy were getting shoes for school. I had the house to myself.

Well, almost to myself. Athena was still there. I heard her nails hit the floor as she jumped off the couch and ran to greet me. She danced around my ankles with the kind of smile that only a welcoming dog can achieve.

"Were you on the couch?" I asked, lecturing her in tender baby-talk. "Were you sneaking in a little nap up there?"

She pushed between my legs and circled back around without ever losing contact, her tail whipping from side to side.

"You think you're sneaky, but I bet if I go over there your beautiful gold fur will be all over it, huh?" I pet her head and loved on her for a moment. "You just leave too much evidence."

She followed me up the stairs and into my room.

"Wanna come up?" I said, patting my bed. "Come on, come up."

Athena jumped onto my bed and circled once before plopping down onto one my pillows. I had a feeling I would find dog fur on my things for the rest of my life.

"You silly girl," I said, stroking her head and down her neck. She was a great dog, but she shed so much I was surprised she wasn't going bald. A clump of fur collected on my hand and clung to my bed sheet as I pet her, but I didn't care much. I'd missed her while I was away at school.

I gave her one last pat before standing up to check my email. She stayed seated on my bed as I slowly walked over to my computer and sat down.

Seeing Caroline, plus everything else that had happened in the past forty-eight hours, had left me in a great mood. Instead of feeling heavy as I checked my email, I was content and comfortable with my shoulders slouched against the back of my chair.

My mind was barely on my email as I scrolled through it. I was thinking of Jacob and what our life could look like together. It was still early in our relationship, but I knew deep in my bones that we were a good match. We could be the real deal.

I decided I should look for some remote-site work. There had to be plenty of jobs I could do on my computer from home until I found something. And working from home would mean I could work from Jacob's home, too. I rather liked the idea of never having to leave his apartment.

I liked the way the future was shaping up. If I found some computer work, I could move out of my parents' house and into one of the apartments on the west side of town. They wouldn't be as nice as Jacob's, but it would be my own. The future was bright.

I opened up a new window and started searching, finding several opportunities that sounded like they would at least open up some doors. For the first time in weeks, I was actually enjoying sending out resumes. I was looking forward to a new career and seeing where things with Jacob went. The world looked bright and promising, and I couldn't wait for it to all happen.

A message beeped that I had new mail. It only took a moment to switch windows to see what it was.

I opened my email account and froze. Sitting at the top of my inbox was the email I had been waiting for.

ZephTech.

I sat forward, my shoulders tense. My fingers melted into my computer mouse and refused to move. Had I not been sitting, my legs would have crumbled under the anxiety in my stomach.

My future plans wavered. This could change everything.

After a deep breath and a concerted effort to collect myself, I opened the email.

CHAPTER 11

*I*n that moment, there were so many things that I never would've anticipated. For one, I'd always imagined waiting restlessly by the computer continuously clicking to refresh my email until the message came. I didn't expect the news to come like a wrench abruptly thrown into a spinning fan.

Either that, or I'd envisioned waking up to the email, something like a kid waking to find that the tooth fairy had visited her pillow the night before. I'd made it out to be a fairytale where promptly after receiving the news I'd run and shout it to whoever would listen.

I'd certainly never imagined feeling regret. Never regret. Excitement, wonder, exultation, amazement- never regret. I never imagined there would be *anything* to make me think twice about the decision.

But then, I'd never imagined finding someone like Jacob and knowing I would need to leave him behind to pursue my dreams.

The email was still up and staring back at me, the words, '*Congratulations*' in big block letters colored bright neon green—ZephTech's signature color—at the top of the page.

I guess I'd expected the email to look a little different too.

I stood up on shaky legs and then sank into my bed, my face falling into my pillows and my arm down onto Athena. The pillows were firm and suffocating until I finally turned my head to the side, looking for air. I took several deep breaths while running my hand through Athena's fur, up and down her back. She was the only thing anchoring me in the real world.

The rest of my mind was gone, detached from my body and drifting in a warp of anxiety. Even my desk chair hadn't felt like enough to keep me from falling through the floor, like the ground itself was collapsing around me.

I felt so many things. Too many to process.

My stomach was empty, but my chest was inflated. Paralyzing anxiety and thrilling excitement were dueling it out in each of my limbs, each feeling winning for moments at a time before changing over completely.

It was nothing like what I thought I'd feel like.

I remained buried in my bed for several minutes—maybe five, maybe twenty—before rolling over and onto my back, but even then I laid still for a while longer. I looked at nothing but a singular spot on my ceiling, seeing nothing and seeing everything all at once; my future, my father's excited face, everything it's taken to get where I was, the countless resumes, *Jacob.*

He hates Silicon Valley, I thought. *He won't come visit me there.*

From across the room I could still see the email up on my computer. My eyes ran down the page again, scanning words in groups instead of individually.

"CONGRATULATIONS. We're pleased to inform you that you've been accepted as an Intern to ZephTech Co. Based on your academic history as well as your learned skills and inherent qualities, we believe you'd be a good fit and would like to extend an offer to join our team."

EMBEDDED in the message was a phone number and instructions to call and follow up with the offer within forty-eight hours.

Forty-eight hours, I thought. I'd waited years for this opportunity and now that I was down to just forty-eight hours, my only wish was that the clock would stop moving.

Why do I even need forty-eight hours? I thought. *Forty-eight hours for what? To make a decision? What decision is there left to make? This is my dream.*

But doubt lingered.

Perhaps that was the biggest surprise of all; I'd never imagined having to decide between my dream job and my dream guy.

FOR THE NEXT four hours I watched episodes of *House Hunters* in the living room. I wanted something to take my mind off of things. Something that would keep me from obsessing over my job and what that meant about my future with Jacob.

It was seven-thirty by the time my father, mother and

Tommy all got home from dinner. I'd seen more houses on TV than I'd ever even been inside in real life.

"Hey, Sweets," my mom said, kissing the top of my head as she came in.

"Hey, Mom," I replied.

"You thinking of buying a house in Boca Raton?" she said, stopping behind me and noting the setting of the episode I was watching.

I faked a laugh, but otherwise ignored her comment. "Did you guys see a movie today?" I asked.

"Yeah, your brother and I saw that new sci-fi one," she said, her attention more on the show than answering the question. "The one with the robots."

"How was it?" I asked, not really caring what the answer was but making conversation anyway.

"It was a little much for my taste, but ask your brother." She shrugged. "I think he liked it."

Tommy walked in and rolled his eyes at my TV program choice. He tucked a shoe box under his arm and headed upstairs to put it away.

"How was your day today?" my father asked, coming in last and shutting the garage door behind him.

"Good," I said, waiting for the inevitable follow-up. My heart was sinking and soaring at the same time.

"How'd your breakfast with Caroline go?" my mother chimed in. Not the follow-up I was expecting.

"It was good," I said with a shrug. "As always."

"Are you doing okay?" my father asked. "You look like you might be sick."

"I've actually got some big news," I said, shifting around in the couch to face my parents. My father was milling around with the mail on the counter and my mother was still watching my TV show. Both of them perked up, both likely anticipating the same news.

"I heard back from ZephTech today," I said. I was surprised my voice stayed steady when I felt like it should crumble to pieces. "They offered me a slot as an intern."

At once both parents uttered different shrieks of excitement that together sounded like the shouts of a playground.

I stood when I realized they were coming over for a hug and I embraced them both at the same time. My father was the first to offer a coherent sentence.

"Good job, sweetie," he said. "Good job." And when he released me and I saw the enormous smile engulfing his face I smiled too. There was a proud shimmer in his eyes as he beamed down at me.

It was the first pure happiness I'd felt all day.

"I'm so, *so,* proud of you baby," my mom said. "You deserve it."

"You really do," my father said. "All your hard work. You've got to be ecstatic."

"Yeah," I said, not completely lying but also not entirely sure what I was feeling. Jacob was still weighing heavily on my mind.

"I wish you'd have come to dinner with us," my mother said. "We could have celebrated."

"We're going to be celebrating this one for a long time," my father assured her, his smile still high in his cheeks.

"Tommy," my mother cried, summoning him to the living room. "You've got to tell your brother."

"Tommy, I got that internship with the app company," I said as Tommy descended the stairs.

"You did?" He paused at the top of the stairs.

"I did." I shrugged and gave a small grin. The news was

finally starting to sink in for me. Their excitement was making it real.

"Congratulations!" he said, pumping his fist in the air. He grinned as he came over to give me a hug. "Does this mean that you've gotta move now?" he asked and instantly I locked up. Tommy released me from our hug as he felt my embrace go weak.

"I don't know," I stammered. The initial euphoria of telling my parents had worn off and now I was back to trying to figure out what to do about Jacob.

"Yeah, guess we've gotta start looking for places in Silicon Valley," my father said and I was glad for it because my stomach was still too heavy and my mind too fuzzy to find a response.

"How exciting," said my mother.

Tommy was the only one waiting on a real response. I pulled my eyes away from a blank stare and met Tommy's gaze, holding it for a moment before speaking.

"Yeah, buddy," I said. "Means I've gotta move."

He'd known the answer but was waiting for me to speak before unleashing a frown across his face.

"That sucks," he said bluntly. "I liked having you here. It wasn't so lonely."

"Yeah, you're telling me," I said, more sincerely than he even realized.

It was almost nine-o'clock when I was finally able to escape from the congratulatory circus I'd found myself in. My room was dark except for the light from my computer still with the email sitting on the screen like a statue. Whether it was a heroic statue or more of a memorial, I couldn't decide.

All I knew was that I had to call Caroline.

I stripped from my clothes and threw on my most

comfortable pajamas. They were old and worn, but familiar and safe.

With a deep breath, I hit Caroline's picture on my screen. The phone rang all the way until voicemail.

I stared at my ceiling fan, watching it spin all the way until I heard the electronic prompt to leave a voicemail. I hung up and immediately dialed again.

This time she picked up after several rings.

"What's up Alicia?" she asked, as if nothing were wrong in the world.

I sucked in a deep breath and then just blurted out what I had to say as quickly as possible. "I got the internship with ZephTech."

"You did?" Caroline's voice squeaked with excitement.

"I did."

"Alicia! That's awesome," she cried out. I could feel her smile through the phone.

"Thanks, Caroline."

"Damn, I'm so freakin' proud of you, girl," she said. "I knew you'd get it. I really did. That's so awesome."

"I know," I said. "It's crazy, right?"

"It's crazy that it's finally real," she said. "But not crazy that you got the job. I freaking knew you would. You've got to be stoked right now."

"Yeah, stoked."

"What's wrong?" Caroline asked, immediately picking up on tone. "What's the problem? Who do I need to beat up for you?"

"Caroline, I'm kind of freaking out," I said. My voice cracked with the effort to keep my emotions in check. "I don't know what I'm going to do."

"What do you mean?" Caroline asked. "Why wouldn't you take the job?"

"Well, okay, so say I take the job and move to Silicon Valley and everything. What about Jacob?" I said, tasting the bitterness of the words as the left my lips. "What are we going to do?"

"Oh, I see," she said, sensing my anxiety for the first time. "You're afraid to tell him?"

"I'm terrified," I said. "But not just to tell him, I'm scared of what's going to happen to the first legit thing I've had with someone in a *long* time."

"You know, just because you got the job doesn't mean you can't still date the guy," Caroline said reasonably.

"But it kind of does," I replied. "He hates Silicon Valley and this internship is intense. It's eighty hour weeks every week. It's sleeping under your desk for two hours before drinking more coffee to keep going. They specifically mention in the application that this is not for people who have families or responsibilities outside of work."

"Remind me why you want this job again?" Caroline replied sarcastically.

"Because it gets me in the door for every job I could ever want," I reminded her. "Plus, it's at the company I want to work for. I'd probably be sleeping there anyway if I could. It's everything I've ever wanted."

"Except Jacob," Caroline added. "So, basically, if you take this job, you're going to disappear off the face of the earth for as long as the internship is, right?"

"Right." I closed my eyes. "If I take this job, all social options are off."

"He does know about the job, right?" she asked after a moment.

"Kind of," I said. "He knows *of* the job. He knows I applied."

"Does he know how bad you *want* it?" she asked. "That it's your dream job?"

"Yeah, he does." I fiddled with a loose thread on my pajamas. The seam on the bottom of my shirt was starting to fall apart.

"Well, that's that," she said as if that settled things. "He can't really expect you to pass up on your dream job offer."

"I don't know what he expects," I said. "But I don't know what I expect either. I don't know what to do."

"You've gotta do what's right for you," she said. "That's all you can ever really do."

"It just doesn't really feel right ending things between us right now. This is the best guy I've ever met. *Ever.*" I sighed and tugged at the thread. It just made more thread come out. "And now I'm just supposed to say, 'sorry, goodbye, I'm on to bigger and better things?'"

"But you are," Caroline said gently. "Nothing says that you're supposed to become a hermit and settle when you're twenty-three years old. You're allowed to pursue your ambitions. You don't have to compromise. You *shouldn't* compromise."

"The thing is, this doesn't even feel like compromising," I said. "I feel torn."

"That's okay though," she said. "Feeling torn is okay but don't let it discourage you."

"I know it sounds stupid or silly or whatever," I said. "But I feel like I'm passing up on something that could be just as important as my dream career, in the grand scheme of things. I feel like I could be passing up on my dream guy."

"Okay. Hold up," Caroline began. "No offense, but you guys have known each other for all of a week or two. If there were wedding plans on the table, or kids or anything like that, it'd be different. But I haven't even been introduced to this guy—which is fine—I'm just saying, you can't really be debating turning down an opportunity like this for a guy that you just met while living at home for a few weeks."

I didn't want to speak, didn't want to confront her comment. It was the same thing I'd been telling myself all day, but still it hadn't stuck. Still there was a barrier preventing the notion from making its way into my head and restoring a sense of rational thought, no matter how badly I needed it.

No matter how much I recognized the logic behind what Caroline had articulated, the barrier remained. My wavering and painful uncertainty remained. I felt something for Jacob that I wasn't ready to give up yet.

"Alicia? You still there?" Caroline asked after a moment.

"Yeah, I'm still here," I said. "Stuck between a rock and a hard place."

"I think you're just stuck between your head and your heart," Caroline said. "And not even *really* that, because your heart wants this job too."

"Does it?" I asked, uncertain of my own thoughts.

"Yes. Just because it's been fun doesn't mean it's your future." She paused. "And it certainly doesn't mean you should disrupt your future, that's for sure."

"What if Jacob *is* my future?" I asked, needing to get the question asked.

There was silence. The words were like tangible objects I had thrown at Caroline and I was waiting to see if they'd hit or if she'd simply dodged them in disbelief. What's worse, I could no longer tell if I was trying to convince Caroline or myself.

"I don't think that's the case," she finally said, carefully selecting her words. "And if your relationship can't survive being apart for a little while, was it really meant to be?"

I didn't want to answer that. I didn't like the implications.

"I really don't think you want to throw everything away for a fling," Caroline quietly said after a moment of silence.

"Yeah," I said, not feeling like I could muster any more than that.

"Don't overthink it," she said. "Be happy for yourself, Alicia. You earned this. No more self-pity and unnecessary confusion. Tell yourself the truth. I want to hear you say it. Tell yourself, 'congratulations' right now."

"Congratulations?"

"No, say, 'CONGRATULATIONS Alicia!'" she commanded. "I want to hear you say it."

"*Congratulations Alicia,*" I repeated, feeling effectively patronized and at the mercy of Caroline's intuition. I was unable to defend myself any more than I'd already tried.

"Good enough," she replied. "Remind yourself of that whenever you feel yourself slipping back into that spiral of nervousness. It's okay to be a little anxious, but don't second guess yourself."

I knew she was right, but I didn't want to let go of my dreams with Jacob just yet. When I had been sure I was never going to get the ZephTech internship, I had convinced myself that Jacob was my future. And those dreams were still dancing through my mind. They were still so beautiful and perfect that I wasn't ready to give them up yet.

"I love you girl," Caroline said, realizing I was drifting into despondence. "Don't forget that either."

"I love you, too," I said. "Thanks for talking to me."

"Of course babe, don't even mention it," she said. "Always here for ya. Just hope I was able to help a little."

"You did," I said, not really sure if I was lying or not.

"It's definitely a big deal," she said. "A big decision. I just think you should approach it with the excitement you deserve."

"It is a big decision," I agreed.

"It's the decision you've been waiting *years* for," she said. "When you're laying in bed thinking about it before you fall asleep, don't think about Jacob or any of the other excuses out there. Think of all the tests, the projects, all the hours you had to put in to get here."

"You're right," I said. There was no doubt that her logic was bulletproof but it was becoming equally as exhausting. Everything was exhausting. "I know you're right. I just need a little bit of time, I guess."

"Okay, well I'll let you get that sleep now," she said. "Give me a call after you tell Jacob, let me know how it goes."

"Okay," I said, not really swallowing what she'd said. I hung up the phone and stared into the dark of my room.

I recognized at least a hint of anger still running in my chest after the phone call, the only part of me that was moving as I stared into the ceiling. The rest of my body was lifeless.

I couldn't believe she could brush off my emotions around Jacob. How could she not know that he lit up my world and made the sky blue again for me? That when I was with him, I was the happiest I'd ever been in my life?

Because you've only known him two weeks and this isn't a fairy-tale, came my own thoughts. *Because she hasn't met him or fallen in love like this before.*

I could clearly see my future as two paths before me. On one, I was working at ZephTech, following my computer dreams. On the other, I was with Jacob and eating picnics in the park.

I wished I could merge the two options together, but my mind refused to combine them. Jacob hated Silicon Valley and as such, if I took this internship, I wouldn't see him for six weeks. Could our relationship survive that? It was still so early in our story together that I wasn't sure.

But, if it's love- it will work, right? I asked myself. I was afraid of the answer, because even though I was in love with him, we hadn't made anything official. I could all too easily see the two of us drifting apart because we never had enough time to make sure our ties were really strong enough to keep us together. There were married couples that fell apart after six weeks of being apart. If they couldn't do it, how in the world could we?

I no longer knew if I was making any sense or confusing myself even more. *But I guess I do know one thing,* I told myself. *I've got to tell Jacob.*

I remembered the way Caroline had told me to *let her know* how breaking the news to Jacob went over, as if chaos were inevitable. *How had she managed to be so excited and skeptical at the same time?* I thought, picturing her lecturing me with her feet up while I lay anguished in my bed.

I had to tell him. But I couldn't tell him over the phone. I reached over, typing and deleting a dozen texts before finally settling on:

 Hey, let's get lunch tomorrow

CHAPTER 12

*M*y head was turned over my shoulder as I edged the corners of my car into the spot behind a truck and in front of a bulky Jeep Rubicon. It was tight, but going to school in Los Angeles had allotted me near professional parallel parking skills.

I'd driven myself on my own suggestion. It didn't feel right asking Jacob to pick me up for a lunch where I'd then profess that I was moving away to take a job that would have me not only in another city, but working crazy hours.

Driving myself eliminated the car ride back, which I figured was destined to be some level of awkward. I really had no idea how the news would go over, whether it would be significant like Caroline had alluded to, or if he'd simply say, "okay, nice knowing you," before politely shaking my hand goodbye. This way, I eliminated any awkward drives home.

It was noon-thirty and the morning warmth was beginning to transition into the heat of the day. I could feel it immediately after stepping out from my Focus and onto the dry pavement. The miniature strip mall that lined the street was already scattered with people, some carrying shopping bags while others held the hands of small children. The block was a cute bundle of stores, coffee shops and small diners.

I'd suggested a quaint, little family owned diner on the corner of the street. It looked almost like a 1950's barbershop, minus the red and white pole, with a canvas extending from the roof to shadow the outside patio. It was a spot I'd been a few times before, renowned for their sandwiches that had become self-asserted as 'The Best Sandwiches in California.'

My palms were sweaty as I walked up. Already the situation had played itself out numerous times in my head, sometimes ending well, others times ending poorly, but never ending in a way that expelled my anxiety and left me feeling ready. Instead, I carried a tremor in my stomach and a heavy angst on my shoulders that had made each step I'd taken that day move just a little bit slower than normal.

I sat down at a two-person metal table designed for the outdoors with a red, plastic tablecloth drawn over the top. Being near the back edge of the patio, my back was to the indoor portion of the diner with a surrounding view of the street in front of me. The perfect spot.

I was taking the internship. There was no reason for me not to. It was my dream and I decided that Jacob could either join in that dream or not. But that choice was now up to him. He had to choose to stay with me for the next six weeks without being able to really see me.

But, if he didn't think he could make it through the next six weeks, then it wasn't going to happen. This would be the cleanest breaking point we could ask for. Dread welled up in my stomach at the thought of him wanting to call it quits because it was going to be hard.

"*You've known each other for a week or two,*" Caroline had said, and perhaps it really was ridiculous to feel as strong as I did after so little time. I imagined Caroline on my shoulder, guiding my thoughts as I sat in preparation. She was right, I knew she was, but it didn't make the moment any easier.

As I sat there, I realized that I'd never really seen Jacob angry. I'd never seen him disappointed. Our interactions together had never made that necessary. We'd never even argued.

And perhaps that's evidence that I don't actually know him that well, I thought. *Perhaps Caroline was right.*

We just hadn't had that much time together. Even though I knew deep in my bones that I was supposed to be with him, the truth was that we needed more time. And that was why I was so nervous. How this meeting went would determine if we had more time together or if we were calling it quits.

I caught a glimpse of Jacob's sporty little car stopped at the light on the next block and my heart skipped a beat. He drove through the light and neared the diner moving slowly, probably looking for parking. With nothing available he turned through the next light and rounded the corner.

Down to a few minutes now, I thought to myself and checked the time on my phone. It was twelve thirty-nine, he was six minutes early for our twelve forty-five lunch, just as I'd expected.

He had a bounce in his step as he approached the restaurant, which only made my stomach twist even more. He looked happy, among other things. Happy and strikingly handsome.

He had a casual look about him, a look that was far different from the attire he'd worn to our dinner but still gave him an air of confidence. He wore his dark-framed glasses that framed his face so well and his t-shirt was a light blue polo, the kind that could be worn whether golfing or lounging at the park. It was the perfect color to bring out his eyes, I thought. Just like every color.

Everything brought out his eyes, the same eyes that would consume me from across the table when I tried to explain my predicament. I already feared it.

He neared the diner and instantly I was glad for not having selected a table on the street side of the patio. The hostess smiled as he came in and I watched through the windows as they exchanged a few words before she pointed him to our table outside. His eyes focused on me as he waved and my stomach tightened responsively as I waved back.

"Good morning," he said as he took his seat across from me. "Or, good afternoon, I should say."

"Hey," I replied, and tried to force a smile until it became effortless as he beamed back at me.

Jacob's eyes scanned the table. "You haven't been waiting awhile, have you? You could've ordered something."

"Oh, no. I just got here maybe a minute before you," I lied, not wanting to look silly.

"Okay, if you say so," he said, his smile crinkling the corners of his eyes. "This looks like a nice place."

"It is, though not compared to the place you picked," I said, looking around at the casual decor.

"It's got its own kind of charm," he said quickly and with a smile. "Plus, I love sandwiches and the sign outside says they are the best."

"Well, fair warning, I don't know if they're the *best* sandwiches in California," I replied. My nerves were making me contrary. I took a deep breath and smiled. "They are good, though."

"Wow. No faith. No hometown spirit." He shook his head in mock disapproval.

I started to giggle and had to stop myself. If I got too drawn in I knew I'd wimp out of breaking the news. This would be when he would decide if he was interested in putting in the effort, or if a clean break was best. I was so hoping for him to want to try.

Our waitress came carrying water a few minutes after Jacob had sat down. I already knew what I'd get—a BLT with avocado, the same thing I always got—so I studied Jacob's face instead of the menu, hoping he'd also made up his mind, anything to expedite the lunch.

"And for you, sir?" the waitress asked, turning to Jacob after she'd scribbled my order on her notepad. His eyes were still jumping around his menu but it hadn't stopped me from telling the waitress we were ready to order.

"I'll also have a BLT with avocado as well," he said after a short beat, deferring to my selection.

"Very good," the waitress replied. She had stringy blond hair and a face that had molded from years of working as a server. "I'll be right back with your orders. Any coffee or tea to go along with your water?"

"I'm fine, thank you," I said quickly.

"No thanks," Jacob said.

Both of us sat quietly for a few moments after she left. Jacob looked to be enjoying the pleasantry of the warm day while I continued to mull over the right words to use.

"So, how have you been since I saw you last?" he asked

with a chuckle. "I know forty-eight hours can be a long time. "

"You're right about that," I said without doing the math. "I've been good, though."

Say it, I thought. *Tell him what's happened in the last forty-eight hours.*

Yet, somehow the words didn't leave my mouth. I wasn't ready to ask him where we stood as a couple yet.

It was only a short while before our waitress returned carrying our food, but not much had been said on either side. We'd traded greetings, commented on the nice weather and debated the best sandwich toppings. It wasn't that he was awkward, but even after the food had been delivered I found myself struggling to keep up with the conversation, as if each reply had to navigate through a sea of fog before finding its way to my lips.

I ate my food, but barely tasted it. I was so nervous. If we were going to break up, this was the moment. This was when it would happen.

With each sentence I was only delaying the inevitable. Everything I said felt out of place, like I was concealing a wound with bandage after bandage. There weren't many things capable of spoiling a good sandwich for me, but sitting across from Jacob with the feeling of impending disaster was one of them.

There were several times, a few hesitations, where I'd tried to pull the words out from my throat but couldn't. Each time I'd stopped myself, not wanting to take the step that would shatter our relationship, or our bond, or whatever it could be called. I didn't want to say the words that could shatter *us.*

But the last thing I wanted was for him to propose

another date. Or to ask how my job search was going. No, the news had to come out on my own accord.

Nothing had changed in my mindset but at the next lull in the conversation there was something that finally pushed the words off my tongue.

"Hey, so, remember that internship I told you about?" I said, the words coming out so fast that I couldn't have stopped myself if I tried.

"Yeah, the one at ZephTech? The really crazy hard one?" Of course he remembered. This was a guy that actually *cared* about me, my goals and my interests, the exact reason that the moment at hand was so difficult.

"Yeah, that one. Well, I kind of have some news," I said, watching his eyes for a reaction. "I got accepted into their internship program."

This was the moment I'd been waiting for. The moment I'd been dreading.

"You did?" he said, his eyes finally reacting with an animated flutter.

I nodded with a forced grin, a signal that I was still awaiting a reaction.

"Alicia! Congratulations," his response sounded exactly like Caroline's. "That's incredible."

"Thank you." I still wasn't sure what was happening yet.

"You got it. You did it." He looked so excited for me, I thought he might jump up and dance around the table.

"Yeah, this is the one I was hoping for," I replied.

"Congratulations," he said enthusiastically. "Lunch is on me."

An enormous smile occupied the entirety of his face. It rose into his cheeks and lifted his bright blue eyes, but still I was lost in my interpretation. There was no bitterness, not even a hesitation in any of his responses. He seemed truly delighted.

"You can't use this as an excuse to pay for something *else*," I said, allowing myself to slightly relax for the first time all day. Being immersed in Jacob's charisma was like medicine.

After a few short seconds I became tense again. I still hadn't even really gotten to the hard part.

"What's wrong?" he asked, his brows coming together. "You should be dancing on the table, but you look about ready to pass out."

"I don't know," I said, trying to stall and move forward at the same time. "It means that I'll have to move away."

"The job's in Silicon Valley, isn't it?" he asked.

"Yeah, it is." I nodded.

"That'll be good for you," he replied. "I bet you'll thrive up there. It's a great place for people interested in computers."

"I hope so," I said, biting my lip. "It's kind of intimidating and I'm just not sure I should take it."

"But it's what you've always wanted," he said. He reached out and touched my hand with his. The touch grounded and terrified me at the same time.

"Yeah, it is," I agreed. I picked up an empty straw wrapper on the table and began fidgeting with it.

"Getting a chance to follow your dreams is no small feat," he said. "I'm really happy for you."

"Thanks Jacob," I said, still feeling like we hadn't yet tackled the beast hiding in the shadows. The straw wrapper tangled and twisted in my fingers. "But..."

"*But* what?" he asked, setting down his food and studying me.

"Well," I began. The straw wrapper ripped between my fingers. "What does this mean for... for *us?*"

"You're asking if you moving away and taking a demanding job changes things between us?" he asked. I was so nervous I couldn't read the tone of his voice.

"Yeah," I said softly, as if speaking too forcefully might jeopardize his response. I stared at my broken straw wrapper, afraid of what he might say next.

"Do you want it to?" he asked. The quiet pain of the question made me raise my eyes to his in an instant.

"No," I said without even having to think. I looked up to meet his eyes. "It's the last thing I want."

"I don't want it to, either," he assured me. "I don't want to lose you, that's for sure."

For a moment I marveled at that. At the way he'd said, '*don't want to lose you.*' The words were like the first crack of sun through heavy clouds. Jacob had done it again.

"I don't want to lose you either," I said, hope that didn't feel foolish building in my chest for the first time.

"Really?" I held my breath, needing him to actually say that we weren't breaking up. "You still want to date me even though I'll be insanely busy for the next two months?"

"Really," he assured me. "Now that I've found you, I'm not letting you go."

My heart was still fluttering, but now it was for an entirely different reason than it was five minutes ago. We were a couple. He didn't want to break up, even though I was going to be leaving. He wanted to try and make it work. Suddenly, all my worrying seemed to be for nothing and I felt a little bit silly.

"I'm sure it's the start to a wonderful career," he said, grinning like he was the one who had just got his dream job.

"It's going to be amazing. It's going to open up so many wonderful opportunities for you."

"Yeah, I can't even think that far right now," I replied with a shrug. "I still have to make it through the intern program before I'm even offered a full-time position. And it's a killer of a program."

"Would you ever consider working for a different company down there in the Valley?" he asked. "A different game developer, maybe?"

"I don't know," I said with a shrug. "I mean, probably. But it's hard to think like that right now. I've literally wanted *this* job ever since I realized I wanted to work in computer programming."

"I guess it's good to have that kind of conviction," he said, slowly. He pushed his glasses up higher on his nose and smiled at me. "I bet you none of the other interns could say that. They're all probably hot shot grads just looking for the best opportunity they can find."

"There's going to be some heated competition," I agreed. "But, I want this job so bad."

"You're going to do great," he said knowingly.

"Thank you," I said, feeling a weight lift off of my shoulders. For the first time since getting the news, I felt like I could be excited. I wasn't going to be forced to choose between my dream job and my dream guy. I could have both.

"I think we should celebrate," Jacob said as we walked out from the diner, hand in hand.

"Ha, that's funny. That's what everyone's been saying," I said. "I guess I just feel like I don't *really* have anything to celebrate quite yet. The hardest part is still ahead of me."

"You've gotta appreciate the little things though," he said. "They're what turns into the big things. You wouldn't be in position to compete for your dream job if you hadn't first been accepted."

"That's true," I agreed. "It is an honor just to be accepted."

"So, come on." We'd paused momentarily after leaving the diner but Jacob tugged my hand away from my car and in the direction of where he'd parked. "I'll drive," he said. "We can come back to get your car later."

"Where are we going?" I asked.

"Back to my place," he said. "To *celebrate.*"

CHAPTER 13

S ix weeks later...

THE SUN HAD SET a long time ago when I finally parked my car in front of my apartment. Wearily, I stepped out of the driver's side door and made my way up the concrete steps that led to the building. My eyes were half closed, as if my body was already anticipating the sleep that it so badly needed.

As soon as I unlocked the door to my place, I noticed that the TV was on in the corner. It was the only light in the room, and it coated the walls with a flickering blue glow. On the couch nearby, was Lauren, my only roommate. She appeared to be sound asleep, with her hands folded underneath her head, using them as a pillow.

Quietly, I closed the front door and locked it before tiptoeing to my bedroom. My bed was tucked in the corner, beckoning me toward it and I didn't hesitate to oblige. I slipped off my skirt suit and changed into some sweat pants and a loose-fitting t-shirt. Then I crawled under my covers, wrapping myself in a cocoon made out of my blankets.

I've been counting down the minutes today, waiting until I could crawl into this bed, I thought. *I don't think I've ever been this tired before.*

What was supposed to have been a ten-hour workday at ZephTech had turned into fourteen. I would have said that I was exhausted, but that word just didn't do any justice to the way I felt. I was drained, depleted and so tired that the bags under my eyes had their own bags.

The competition between the interns at ZephTech had made for the toughest six weeks of my life. It was much more intense than I could have imagined. The ten of us that were chosen for the internship had been given just six weeks to create an app that would impress the company. Whoever created the best one would win a full-time position at Zephtech. The owner and CEO of the company, Steve Lynchell, would be the final judge to decide which of the submitted programs was the best.

When I left home, I had thought for sure that it would be a piece of cake. I had a programming degree, loved being creative and considered myself to be an extremely hard worker. But I didn't realize just how smart, aggressive and competitive the other qualifying interns would be. Before I came to Silicon Valley, I had thought of myself as an above average programmer. But after a competition like this, I learned that I was nobody special. I was going to have to work harder than ever just to have a fleeting chance of being noticed. Amazing software engineers were a dime a dozen in The Valley.

But none of that mattered now. I had given it my absolute best and the competition was officially out of my hands. The six weeks were up and I had finally submitted my final program. Mr. Lynchell would be reviewing all of the submissions first thing the next morning. Soon would be my moment of truth. I'd find out if the dating app I had created would be good enough to make me stand out among the other interns.

Not only had it been six weeks of non-stop grinding work, though. It had also been six weeks without seeing my family or Jacob. They were on my mind constantly. I missed them more than I ever thought I could.

I knew I should get up and at least brush my teeth and take my birth control pills, but I was so tired, I couldn't get the energy to do it. I felt bad that I'd gotten off my schedule with my birth control, but since Jacob wasn't here, it wasn't too big of an issue. I needed to get to the pharmacy since the last time I went was right before graduation.

My cell phone rang on my nightstand and I looked over, squinting my eyes against the bright light from the screen. As if he had read my mind, Jacob was calling for our nightly conversation. His call was the highlight of my day every day and was the thing I looked forward to most. I quickly reached over and answered it.

"Hey," I said, barely stopping a yawn.

"Hey, gorgeous," he said. I could hear the smile in his voice. "How are you doing?"

I rolled over onto my back and stared at the ceiling. I wasn't too sure how to answer the question. The truth was that I was a hot mess. I felt more like a zombie than I did a human and what I really wanted right then was to cuddle up with Jacob and fall asleep.

"I'm okay, I guess," I said, omitting much of how I really felt.

"You don't sound like it," he said. "Are you feeling okay?"

"Just tired," I said. "It's been a long week. Actually, it's been a long *six weeks*, but this last one has been especially draining."

"Did you get your program finished up for the competition?" he asked.

"I did," I said. "I hope it does well."

"I think it'll do fine. I took another look at the beta version last night for you and I thought it looked great. I highly doubt that the other interns are submitting apps that are both as beautiful-looking *and* as user friendly as yours is."

"I don't know, Jacob. I thought so too, but these Silicon Valley programmers are a different breed of people. I've never met software engineers with this much talent before."

"It's true, there's some serious talent out there," he said. "But I'm confident that you're just as talented, if not more so."

"You're just saying that," I said, not bothering to stop the small smile the compliment elicited.

"No, I really believe it," he said. "I mean the fact that you're my girlfriend maybe makes me a little biased, but I still believe it. You're as smart and as capable as anybody else in the internship. They wouldn't have chosen you for it if that wasn't the case."

He was right, but it didn't keep my mind from churning with doubt.

"I guess we'll see what happens," I said.

"When do you find out who the winner is?" he asked.

"Supposedly tomorrow before noon," I said. "The owner and his colleagues will be looking at the programs starting super early tomorrow morning and they'll make a decision right away. I'm so nervous."

"Speaking of tomorrow, we're still on for getting

together, right?" He paused for a moment. "We can cancel if you aren't feeling up to it."

"Are you kidding me?" I nearly sat straight up, but I was too tired. "Of course we are. I've been waiting all week to see you."

Jacob and I had made plans for him to come out to Silicon Valley to visit me. I knew that he hated coming to Silicon Valley, so the gesture meant the world to me. He'd wanted to come every weekend since I had moved there, but I had been too busy to make it work. Now that the competition was over, though, I finally had time to see him.

"I've really missed you," he said. "I want to kiss you so badly."

"I want to do far more than just kiss you," I informed him. "Those sexts I sent you weren't just me killing time at the office."

He chuckled. "I did enjoy those texts. Particularly the one where you wanted me 'to shudder with ecstasy as I come into you.' I could go for that right now."

"I could go for it, too. What time will you be coming in tomorrow?" I asked. I shifted in bed so the pillow was more comfortable. I could already feel my eyelids starting to droop, but I wanted to talk to Jacob more. Talking to him was the highlight of my day, so I wasn't about to fall asleep on him.

"Probably around three in the afternoon," he said.

"I'm so excited," I said, stifling a yawn. "What would you like to do when you're here?"

"Other than you?" Jacob asked, making me laugh. "Maybe we could go to a nice dinner and just relax. Or you can take me out and show me around your new town. Whatever you want."

"A dinner sounds nice," I said. "But if anybody is going

to be giving a tour around Silicon Valley, it's going to be you. I hardly know of a single interesting destination here, besides the coffee shops that are located between my apartment and the ZephTech building. I haven't had much time to explore. The past six weeks of my life I've only existed in my apartment and my office."

"I'm sorry you've been so busy," he said. "But the tough part is behind you now. Tomorrow we can relax and celebrate. It's time to have some fun."

"I hope that by the time you get here tomorrow I'll have good news from the competition and a reason to celebrate," I said. "I could either be really happy or really disappointed tomorrow afternoon and it all depends on ZephTech's decision."

"I've got a good feeling," he said. "Regardless of what happens, though, tomorrow will be a great day."

"Yes, I guess whether I win the competition or I lose, we'll have a reason to get drinks," I joked.

"That's the spirit," he said. "So I've got to ask, though. Is Silicon Valley everything that you'd hoped it would be?"

"Yes and no," I said. "I love the energy here and the amazing technology. It's one of the only places I've been where being a nerd is actually encouraged. I really like that part. The people seem pretty nice too. But I seriously miss home. Silicon Valley doesn't feel like a place that I could ever call home, you know?"

"Trust me, I understand that completely. There's a reason I don't like going there," he said. "I called it home for a long time, but it never gave me that feeling of 'home'. I've been in here for only a few months and it feels more homey to me than Silicon Valley ever did."

"I agree. Maybe I'm just tired and homesick, but..." I shrugged. "This isn't home yet."

"You miss me?" he asked. I could practically here the flirtatious smile on his voice. "Or just home?"

"God yes, I miss you. I miss everyone, including Athena," I said with a smile. I knew he was just teasing me.

"She's a cute pup, that's for sure," Jacob agreed. "I'm sure she misses you, too."

"I'd like to give her a snuggle," I said. "But not as much as I'd like to cuddle up with you."

"That would be nice right about now," he said. I heard him move something around on his end of the line. "This place definitely isn't the same without you around."

My eyes were getting heavier by the second. It was so nice to hear Jacob's voice and if I had had more energy, I would have stayed awake all night long talking to him. But the long hours at work had taken its toll and sleep was knocking on my door.

"I hate to cut this short, but I think I need to go to bed," I said. I couldn't stop the yawn from escaping this time. "I'm beyond exhausted."

"That's okay," he said. "Get some rest. I'll see you tomorrow afternoon."

"I can't wait," I said.

"Me either," he assured me. I could almost imagine him leaning over and kissing me. "Goodnight."

"Goodnight," I whispered.

I hung up and set my phone on the nightstand. The screen filled the room with a soft glow for a few seconds before it went black. When it did, I closed my eyes and drifted into a deep sleep instantly.

～

I woke up in a panic and ran to my bathroom, flipping up

the lid of the toilet quickly as I dropped to my knees in front of it. Then I threw up, not once but three times, one right after the other. My stomach clenched until it was all over. Once the storm had passed, I laid down on the bathroom floor for a minute. I drew in a long breath and tried to relax. The nausea was gone, but my stomach still felt tight from the throwing up.

Sunlight flickered on the bathroom floor and I shut my eyes against it. All I wanted to do was curl up in a ball and die. There was nothing I hated more than throwing up. It was terrible. The nausea, the retching, the smell. I wanted so badly to avoid it. I thought that maybe a sip of water could make the feeling go away, so I took a drink from the glass next to my sink. It only made it worse, though and my stomach turned again. That water was coming back up, whether I liked it or not.

Dammit, I thought. I closed my eyes and willed the water to stay down. It took a moment of me concentrating only on my breathing and sheer will power, but the need to vomit finally passed.

"Must have been something I ate, I guess," I said to myself, as I slowly stood up and walked back toward my bed.

I had skipped dinner the night before, though, since I had been at work. And for lunch, all I had eaten was a salad. It was hard to imagine that whatever had made me sick was food poisoning.

Oh well. Could just be that the stress of the past six weeks has finally caught up to me, I thought. *Either way, I hope that it's all out of my system now.*

I glanced at the alarm clock on my nightstand, and was surprised to find that it was nearly eleven in the morning.

Wow, I must have been even more tired than I realized, I thought. *I never sleep in this late.*

Jacob would be arriving in a couple of hours, which still gave me plenty of time to get ready. I decided I'd go out to the kitchen and make a cup of coffee before checking my email. When I opened my bedroom door, the smell of fresh-cooked bacon and eggs entered my nose. I nearly ran back to the bathroom to throw up again, but instead just breathed through my mouth. Lauren was standing in front of the stove and she turned to face me with a smile on her face.

"Good morning," she greeted me, raising up her spatula in a wave. "Sleep well?"

I let out another yawn before responding. "I can't believe how late it is, though. You're making breakfast, so I guess I wasn't the only one to sleep in."

"You want some?" she asked, motioning to her cooking. "I've definitely made enough for two."

"No thanks, I'm good," I said, holding my stomach with my hands and trying very hard not to think about food. "I just need some coffee."

Lauren spun around and grabbed a mug from the cupboard. Then she poured me a cup of strong black coffee. She handed it over and I took a sip, but something about it tasted off.

I had to admit that it was nice having a roommate again that wasn't my parents. Especially having a roommate who was as considerate as Lauren. I had found her in the local want ads, where she posted that she was looking for someone to rent out her extra bedroom. It was a perfect situation, because she wasn't concerned about having me sign a lease as long as I agreed to pay the rent on time.

She worked in Silicon Valley as a programmer, but for a different company. She knew how demanding my internship was and she was always super quiet when I was trying to sleep and understood when I wasn't home until weird hours. I couldn't have asked for a better last-minute living situation.

"What are you up to today?" she asked, as she pulled food from the frying pan and situated it neatly on her plate. Just looking at it made me queasy, so I focused on my coffee cup.

"Jacob will be coming to visit in a few hours," I said. I couldn't have stopped the excited smile if I wanted to.

"Oh really?" she asked. "I'll make sure to clear out of the house for a few hours then."

"Thanks. I'm super excited," I said. "But that's not the only thing that's going on. I also get to find out who won the competition at my internship today."

"That is not only exciting, but also terrifying," Lauren said as she took her plate of food and sat at our small dining room table. I followed her over and we took a seat across from each other. "Good luck."

"Tell me about it," I said. "I've spent the last six weeks here working my butt off and I don't have a lot of other job prospects at the moment."

"That's a lot of pressure," she said. "What time do you think you'll find out today?"

"I'm going to check my email as soon finish my coffee," I said. "I'm hoping that the results will be in there. Then I'll know what direction my life is heading. It all hinges on one email. Kind of crazy, huh?"

Lauren nodded. "Welcome to Silicon Valley."

I couldn't help but to laugh. "Yeah, I'm learning that this place will chew you up and spit you out if you're not careful."

"Here's to you winning, then," Lauren said, holding up

her coffee mug. "I don't do well when people cry. It makes me feel awkward. I never know if I should hug them or just walk away."

"Well, I hope I don't cry then," I said. "And if I do, just hug me and hand me a glass of wine. Then you can walk away."

"Nah," she replied shaking her head. "I'll help you at least drink the wine."

I laughed and tried to sip my coffee, but just smelling it made my stomach queasy again.

"Did you do anything different to the coffee this morning?" I asked, examining my cup. I'd barely been able to take more than a mouthful of it. "It tastes weird."

"No," Lauren said, shaking her head. "It's the same stuff as last week. Maybe it's going stale or something? Mine tastes normal."

"I don't know, but I'll just put it in the sink for now. It's time for the moment of truth," I announced as I poured out my cup. "I'm going to go check my email."

"Good luck, Alicia," she said. She held up her hands and crossed all the fingers she could. "You've got this. I know you do."

I hope she's right, I thought, as I walked out of the kitchen and back to my bedroom.

My laptop had finished starting up and I went online and straight to my email. A lump rose in my throat. In my inbox was one unread email and it was from Steven Lynchell. The title of the email said, "Intern's App Development Results".

I held the pointer over the email, hesitating for a moment. My future depended on what was inside and I was terrified to see. No matter what it read, though, there'd be a lot of things changing in my life. With a nervous sigh, I clicked the email and read it.

Dear Alicia Chambers,

I want to tell you personally that I appreciate your participation in the internship challenge. My team and I have been up all evening, reviewing all of the submissions, trying to decide which one we thought was the best. And it was tough. Every single one of the programs that you intern had created for us was excellent and it became clear that everyone had given it their all.

Unfortunately, we only have one full time position currently available at ZephTech; otherwise we'd hire every single one of you. But the good news for you, Alicia, is that you're the one we decided on. My colleagues and myself all agreed that your dating app had the elements we wanted to see. It was beautifully crafted, operated flawlessly and served a purpose. These were the three elements we were judging on and your app passed with flying colors.

Congratulations, Alicia. Welcome to the team. I'll see you Monday to fill out some paperwork. Attached are the conditions of the position. I hope you have an amazing weekend. Looking forward to working with you.

Sincerely,
Steve Lynchell
CEO
ZephTech, Inc.

"No way," I whispered, as I brought my eyes back to the top of the email to re-read it. I figured I must have read it wrong or interpreted it incorrectly.

But the "Congratulations, Alicia" stood out on the page and after looking it over at least five times, I stood up from my chair and let out a squeal.

"I did it!" I called out. "Oh, my God. I did it!"

Lauren busted into my room, her eyes as wide as her smile.

"You won?"

"I won," I told her, finally feeling it start to sink in. "I won the competition!"

She ran up and pulled me in for a hug, practically lifting me off the ground.

"I *knew* you were going to win," she announced, setting me down. "Congrats, Alicia."

Lauren gave me another hug and said, "We'll celebrate more soon, okay? Maybe we can get drinks this weekend."

"Sounds great," I said. "I'm looking forward to it."

She grinned and gave me one more hug. "I'm off to run some errands. Congratulations again!"

She left my room and I closed the door behind her. My hands were trembling from the excitement. I couldn't believe that it was actually happening. Six weeks of hard work had paid off and I had been offered my dream job. I sat on my bed in disbelief. I was beyond excited and proud of myself for what I had accomplished, but I couldn't deny that my feelings were a mixed bag. My entire life was about to change and my new home would soon be Silicon Valley.

I thought about the conversation I had had with Jacob the night before, about how I didn't think I could ever call

The Valley my home. It was true. My real home was where I grew up.

When I took the job, I wouldn't get to see my family or Jacob as often. Maybe I'd take a drive down on a weekend once in a while, but I couldn't imagine that I'd be able to get much time off, at least for the first few months. I would have to look at the job description in the attachment to figure out what I needed to do.

I'll just have to figure out a way to make it work, I thought. *There's no way I'm turning down the job at this point. That's not an option.*

I'd finally be making money and have a secure position with a great company. I'd be able to climb the corporate ladder and move up in the world, something I had wanted to do since I graduated. For the moment, I wasn't going to worry about what was going to happen next. For right now, I was going to be happy I had succeeded.

I grinned and did a little happy dance. I picked up my phone, ready to call Jacob and tell him the good news, but then I changed my mind. It would be so much more fun to tell him in person.

CHAPTER 14

*J*ust five minutes after I stepped out of the shower, someone knocked on the apartment door. My hair was still wet and I was wearing only a towel. I hadn't even had a chance to think about what clothes I wanted to wear for when Jacob got in town later that afternoon.

"Lauren, can you get that?" I called out.

There was no reply, so I walked over to my door and poked my head out into the living room.

"Lauren?"

The apartment was silent and Lauren's bedroom door was open. She was nowhere to be found. I glanced at the clock. It was two in the afternoon and I assumed that she must have gone to the gym or for a run in the park.

There was another knock on the door, this time a little louder and faster than before.

"Hold on. I'm coming!" I said.

Crap, who's here right now? I hope it's not some salesman or something. I'm going to be so pissed if I rushed for that, I thought.

I ran back into my room and dropped my towel, before stepping into some jeans and a t-shirt. My wet hair fell around my face and I did my best to push it away as I walked back to the front door.

Whoever was on the other side continued to knock.

"Geez, give me a *second*," I said, clearly becoming irritated.

I pulled the door open and my attitude changed the instant I saw who was standing on the other side.

"Jacob?" I said, my eyes widening with delight.

He stood there with a bouquet of roses and a smile. He was wearing a white dress shirt and gray slacks. His hair was combed perfectly and he looked as happy as could be.

"Hi, beautiful," he said.

"Oh, my God, Jacob," I squealed, as I lunged toward him. "I can't believe you're here! I thought you weren't getting in until three."

I jumped up and wrapped my arms over his neck.

"There was less traffic than I expected," he said. "Plus, I was driving fast. I wanted to get here as quickly as possible."

Jacob set the roses on the counter and then cradled me in his arms. He gazed into my eyes as he leaned in for a kiss. Our lips collided. It was deep and passionate, the kind of kiss you give someone when you haven't seen them in way too long. We made for a while, before I finally pulled away.

"I missed you," I told him breathlessly.

Jacob set me down on the floor and put his hands on my hips, still holding me close. "I missed you, too. I can't tell you how happy I am to have you in front of me right now."

He leaned forward and kissed me again. I was so happy that he had shown up early, even though I clearly wasn't ready for his arrival. When he pulled back, I reached up and tried to straighten out my hair with my fingers.

"Sorry I look like a total mess," I said. "I just got out of the shower."

"You look beautiful," he said. "As always."

"Can you give me a few minutes to get ready?" I asked.

"Of course. Take your time," he replied. "There's no rush."

"Okay, make yourself at home. The couch is pretty comfy and we have Wi-Fi here. I won't be long," I told him. "I just need to get dressed and put on some makeup."

"Sounds good," he said with a grin.

Jacob stepped over to the living room and plopped down on the couch. I was giddy as I went back to my room to get ready. My strange day, which had started off with me throwing up, was now infinitely better since Jacob was there with me.

I didn't waste much time. I straightened my hair and put on my makeup. Then I got dressed in my best-fitting jeans and silk blue blouse. When I stepped back into the living room, Jacob's eyes lit up.

"Whoa," he said.

I stepped over and sat next to him on the couch. His eyes were still locked on my body. I placed my finger underneath his chin and lifted his face until his gaze met mine.

"Hey, mister. I'm up here," I said, with a playful smile.

"I don't mean to stare, but you look incredible. A sight for sore eyes, that's for sure," he said. "I seriously missed you."

Snuggling next to him on the couch helped to put me at ease. The ball of anxiety and stress that had built inside of me over the previous six weeks was instantly starting to dissolve. His presence was good medicine for me.

"Thanks for coming all the way up here to see me," I said. "Did you have a good drive?"

"Yeah, the drive was good. It went by pretty fast," he replied. "Driving into town wasn't actually as bad as I remember, so that's good."

"I'm so glad you're here." I snuggled into him a little more. "This is the first weekend I've had off from work in a while, so I plan on enjoying it thoroughly."

Jacob's eyes lit up and he faced me. "Speaking of work, did you find out the results of the competition yet?"

"I did," I said. I had to struggle to keep my face straight. I didn't want to give it away yet. It was just too good.

"And...?"

"Let's go get lunch and I'll tell you what happened," I said.

It took a lot of effort, but I managed not to smile. I didn't want to give it away quite yet. I wanted to tell him at lunch about the job offer, that way we could get a proper drink to celebrate.

JACOB HAD FOUND a quaint little café at the end of town to get lunch. It was really cute, with outdoor tables and a huge menu with good-looking food. We had the hostess seat us outside on the patio so we could enjoy the California sun.

"This place is adorable," I said, glancing around and enjoying being out for the first time in weeks.

We sat across from each other and held hands over the top of the table. I hadn't been able to take my eyes off of him since he had arrived.

"You have to try their strawberry and Nutella crepes," he said. "When I lived here, I'd come here at least once a week to order them. Trust me, you won't regret it. It's one of the few things I like around here."

"They sound divine," I said. "I can't wait to taste them."

"I can't wait to taste you," he replied with a smirk. "Why are we at a restaurant again? And not in your bed?"

I chuckled and pushed his shoulder gently. "Because we're waiting for my roommate to leave."

"Right," he said, nodding. "That way you can be loud."

"Shh!" I pushed his shoulder again, a little harder this time as I turned bright red. "The waitress will hear you."

"Oh, well that wouldn't do," he said, shaking his head. He grinned, showing me all his teeth. "Then she'd want to join in, and I'm just not sure I'm ready to share you."

I rolled my eyes at him and pushed him one more time on the shoulder for good measure. "You're trouble."

"You like it," he assured me. I found that I really did.

The waitress came up and Jacob ordered everything, including some appetizers, two grilled cheese and tomato soup combos and of course, the Nutella crepes for dessert. When the girl left, Jacob brought his attention back to me.

"Okay, now that our food is ordered, I want to hear the news," he said. He pushed up his glasses, ready for whatever I was going to tell him.

"What news?" I asked, faking a confused expression.

"Ha, very funny," he said. "Don't leave me in suspense any longer, Alicia. You're killing me."

"I don't know how to tell you," I said, biting my lip and looking away. I deserved an Oscar for this performance.

"Just spill it," he said. "Did you win the competition or not?"

I took a sip from my water, then my lips curled up into a smile. I couldn't contain it any longer.

"I won," I announced.

"You won?"

"Yep. I got the job," I said, nodding and letting my smile free.

"You're kidding me," he said, his eyes widening.

"No, I'm serious, Jacob," I replied. "I got an email this morning from Steve Lynchell himself. He said that my app was the best one out of the bunch. He offered me a full time position with ZephTech."

"Alicia, that's amazing!" He hopped up from his chair and maneuvered around the table. He wrapped both arms around me and squeezed me tight, while kissing me on the cheek. I giggled and turned red, as the other patrons of the restaurant turned to look. He kissed me a few more times and then returned to his seat. I was glowing.

"It's pretty exciting, huh?" I said.

"So exciting. What else did they say in the email?" he asked. His eyes sparkled with excitement for me. "Tell me everything."

"Mr. Lynchell basically said that he thought my dating app had everything that they were looking for. He said it was beautiful, easy to use and served a function. I hit all three nails on the head, apparently."

"See, I told you that your creativity would get you a job," Jacob said, proudly. "I didn't see any of the other entries, but I'm positive that yours looked the best. You did an amazing job, Alicia. I'm so proud of you."

"Thank you," I said. "I'm still kind of in shock about it, honestly. It doesn't even seem real."

"I'll bet," he said. "What does the job look like? What are they going to have you working on?"

"It was in an attachment, so I haven't read it yet." I shrugged and gave him a sheepish smile. "I just kind of wanted to enjoy the high of winning for a little bit before seeing what kind of work I'm in for."

Jacob nodded. "You worked hard and you deserve a little bit of happiness. I'm so proud of you."

I grinned. His approval meant the world to me. "I don't have to sign anything until Monday, so I have the whole weekend to look at contract."

Jacob frowned slightly before pushing at his glasses again. "Be sure you look it over carefully. I've heard some shady things about ZephTech, and I just don't want you to fall prey to them."

"Shady things?" A slight annoyance spiked through me. "And you didn't say anything?"

"I did some research after you got the internship," he admitted. "It's just things like they demand overtime, extra unpaid hours, and the culture is to go above and beyond all the time. Nothing illegal or wrong, just... shady."

My mouth twisted for a moment. I wanted to tell him he was wrong, that my experience at ZephTech had been nothing like that, except it hadn't. That was my experience to a tee. It was the culture there to be available for crazy hours and always be running above and beyond for the love of the company. To be honest, the constant drive for excellence was what had initially attracted me to the company.

"It's what you want, right?" he asked. He smiled gently. "Because, if it's what you want, then I support you."

"Yes, it absolutely is," I replied quickly. "This is the beginning of my career and if I accept the position, then I've got the world open to me. Even if it's a little rough to start."

Jacob placed his hands over mine and squeezed them affectionately.

"I know you know this, but you don't *have* to take the job offer, Alicia," he said.

"You're right, I guess," I said. "But I'm *going* to take it. I need a job and this is my dream job. I'm just nervous for the change."

"Hey, you won't be living that far away from home. It's not like you have to move to the east coast or something," he replied. He shrugged and looked around. "And the drive isn't that bad."

"You promise that we can still see each other?" I asked. "Even if I'm in Silicon Valley and you hate it here?"

"Of course," he assured me. "I'm not going to stop dating you just because you'll be living up here full time. I'll admit, though, that it might be tough sometimes. The past few weeks have been a struggle for me. But we'll make it work. It's worth it."

His words made me feel a lot better about the situation. It suddenly felt a little less daunting.

"Thanks for being so supportive," I said.

"All I care is that you're happy," he said. "I know you want this job, Alicia. It's what you've been working toward for years. Just make sure that what they are offering is what you want. Don't take it just because it's ZephTech. Take it because it's right for you."

"I'll make sure it's what I want," I promised. "But, for now, I want to celebrate."

"Then, I'd say it's time for a celebration drink," Jacob declared.

The waitress had just walked up with our food as Jacob finished speaking. She set our plates down and Jacob turned to face her.

"We have some celebrating to do," he told her. "My beautiful girlfriend here just got offered the job of her dreams."

"How exciting," the waitress said, with a warm smile. "What would you like to drink?"

It was barely after two in the afternoon and my stomach still wasn't feeling all that great from whatever stomach bug I had. I shrugged.

"Ginger ale?" I suggested.

"Whoa, you're serious about this celebration," the waitress said with a wink.

"That's all you want?" Jacob asked, frowning slightly.

"My stomach has been feeling a little off for the past couple of days," I said.

"In that case, we'll take two ginger ales," Jacob said.

"Sounds great," the waitress replied, before turning and leaving to fetch our drinks.

She was back within minutes to hand us our bubbling ginger ale in tall glasses, topped with one of those little umbrellas. I loved that she had made the drink look special.

"Here's to you and your dream job," Jacob said, holding up his ginger ale.

"Thank you, Jacob." I grinned at him.

We clinked our glasses together and took a sip. The carbonation helped to ease my stomach and eating sounded infinitely more appetizing than before.

"So, we'll eat lunch, then what?" Jacob asked. "This is your day."

Truth be told, the only thing I really wanted was to spend time with him. I had been without him for six weeks. That meant no kisses, no sex and no snuggles. We could have spent our time walking our Silicon Valley, but what I really wanted was to have him to myself for a little while. Especially since my roommate was currently away from the apartment.

"Let's go back to my place after we finish here," I said.

His eyes lit up. He knew what was on my mind.

"Sounds like a plan," he said.

CHAPTER 15

*W*e went straight back to my place after lunch. The entire drive over, it was all I could do to keep my hands off of him. I wanted to touch every inch of him and make sure he was still real. That this whole day wasn't just a wonderful dream where I got everything that I wanted.

As soon as he parked the car, I grabbed his hand and led him up the stairs to the front door of my apartment building. For the past six weeks, we'd only been able to talk on the phone. We'd done our share of dirty talk and sexy emails, but it was never as good as the real thing. I wanted to touch him, to taste him- which was just something I couldn't do over the phone or in an email.

As we walked down the hallway toward my apartment, our hands were all over each other. He walked close behind me, burying his face into my neck and grabbing my butt. I'd reach back and playfully touch the front of his slacks, where his bulge had already formed. His every touch sent my senses into overdrive.

I poked my head into my apartment and looked around.

Then I called out for my roommate, just to make sure that she wasn't there.

"Lauren?"

No answer. I grinned.

"Okay, come on," I said, grabbing Jacob's hand again and pulling him into my place.

I tossed my purse and sunglasses carelessly onto the kitchen counter, as Jacob shut the door behind us.

"God, I want you," he muttered, his eyes moving up and down my body. "Get over here."

It wasn't like I needed his encouragement. I was already halfway there and my hands went straight to the buttons on his shirt. Quickly, I undid them. If it hadn't been such an expensive looking shirt, I probably would have just ripped it off to save time.

His hands were all over my body while I worked to remove his shirt. He touched my hips, then wrapped around to squeeze my butt. Then he brought his fingers up the back of my silk dress. By the time he got there, I had undone all of the buttons on his dress shirt. I opened it up and Jacob removed it the rest of the way. He was now shirtless, wearing only slacks and dress shoes. Something about it was super sexy.

"Help me take my top off," I said, as I held my arms into the air.

Jacob growled sexually as he took the bottom of my shirt in his hands and pulled it up over my arms. He tossed it onto the counter-top next to my purse and then immediately began kissing my neck.

I moaned softly, whispering words of want as he caressed me.

Six weeks of not seeing him made his touch that much better and more satisfying. I hadn't realized how much I had missed him until he was there with me. I breathed in deep, savoring the scent of his musk and cologne, bathing in the sensation of his lips on my skin.

Jacob stepped forward and dropped his hands down to my ass. Then he lifted me up and set me on the counter next to the sink. I wrapped my legs around him and cocked my head to the side as he continued to kiss the outside of my neck. It was clear that he wanted this just as badly as I did by the way he never let his fingers leave my skin.

I unclasped my bra and let it fall off of my shoulders. My nipples were already erect, even though he hadn't touched them yet. With my bra now off, though, Jacob began to fondle my breasts, gently sliding his fingers over my hard nipples. He pulled his face away from my neck and then move straight to my chest. He kissed between my cleavage, moaning as he did so. Then his hands slid down my belly, as he brought his lips to one of my nipples. My jaw dropped and I breathed in, as Jacob worked the magic of his tongue on the sensitive nub.

God, I missed this, I thought. We'd had six weeks of fore-play leading up to this moment, and I wanted it more than I wanted to breathe.

He lashed his tongue against my nipple, flicking it gently but rapidly. I placed my hands behind me on the counter and leaned back a little bit. It felt good to just relax and let him pleasure me. It had been way too long.

As he gave attention to my chest, I wrapped my legs around his waist and pulled him closer. Sitting on the counter put his bulge at the same height as my sensitive area. Even through my jeans I could feel the friction as he rubbed against me. It sent a wave of ecstasy pulsing into me, making me want him inside of me even more.

"Jacob, take me," I begged. "Don't wait."

I wasn't afraid to show my eagerness. We had both been so patient over the past six weeks. It was time to let loose.

He pulled his mouth slowly away from my breasts and took a step back. His chest was rising and falling in cadence to his breathing, which had become noticeably heavier in the past few minutes. My eyes moved downward, where they stopped at the bulge in his slacks. I licked my lips when I saw it, practically drooling in anticipation of having it inside of me.

Jacob kept his eyes locked on me while he got undressed. He didn't take his time either. He undid his belt quickly and pulled down his slacks and underwear at the same time. He kicked off his shoes as his pants fell down to his ankles, then he stepped out of the clothing.

I wanted to taste him. I slid off of the counter and dropped to my knees, bringing my hand around the base of his shaft. Jacob let out a moan and leaned his head back, closing his eyes. Slowly, I moved my hand up and down his length, feeling the subtle ridges of his dick each time my grip moved toward his crown.

"Yes," he whispered, bringing his hands to the top of my head.

His tip was only a few inches away from my mouth as I slowly pleasured him with my hand. I looked up at him and then brought my gaze back to his manhood and parted my lips, allowing his crown to slide between them.

"God, yes," he groaned, as his sensitive tip made contact with my tongue.

I opened a little wider, allowing more of his length in. Then I began bobbing my head up and down over him. Each of my movements caused Jacob to grunt in pleasure. I looked up again, and this time our eyes met. He was lost in lust, his pupils completely blown and his lips parted just enough so that he could release his short breaths.

I need him inside of me right now. I feel like I'm going to explode if I don't get it soon, I thought.

Slowly, I pulled my mouth away. Jacob took my hands and helped me back to my feet. Standing there naked in the kitchen, he looked so damn sexy that it drove me crazy. My body was tingling all over and I began to throb desperately.

"We should go to my room," I said. "Just in case my roommate decides to come home."

Jacob nodded and we stepped out of the kitchen into my bedroom, closing the door behind us. We had left our clothes scattered on the kitchen counter, so if Lauren did happen to come home, she would have known what was going on, but I figured it was better than having her walking in on the act itself.

In the privacy of my bedroom, I quickly pulled off my jeans and panties. Then I stepped close to Jacob. His cock slid between my thighs and I shivered as he touched me.

We kissed, and as we did, I found myself slowly bucking my hips forward and back. It made me even wetter, as the movement created a pleasurable friction. I was practically panting when we finally broke the kiss.

Jacob lifted me up and laid me down on the bed, and then crawled over me. I wrapped my legs around his waist and pulled him closer. There was no hesitation on his part as he entered me.

He pressed in, slowly and steadily. I drew in a breath as he inched his way inside, relieving the desperate throb and filling me with ecstasy.

"I missed you so much," he said, looking deep into my eyes.

I lifted my hands above my head and closed my eyes.

The waves of pleasure washed over me, and I savored every second of it. Our bodies were entangled once again, after the longest six weeks of my life. It felt better than any other time we had ever made love.

Jacob continued to thrust as he leaned forward and sucked on my breasts. The combination filled me with even more sensation and soon I was yelping out in cadence to his movements. I felt complete with him there. Complete and lost in a state of bliss, not wanting to ever find my way out.

Jacob varied the speed of his movements, making each pulse of pleasure unique and intense. When I finally opened my eyes, I soaked up the view in front of me. Something about watching Jacob make love to me turned me on even further. It made me feel wanted and special. I was the center of his entire world as we laid on that bed, and that fact felt just as incredible as the sex itself. But as much as I loved watching him, I wanted to feel him in a different position.

"Take me from behind," I said, my words sounding more like a command than a request.

He didn't seem to mind, though. He did as I asked and as soon as he pulled out, I flipped around on the bed and bent over in front of him. The instant I looked back over my shoulder, he grabbed my hips and plunged back inside of me.

I drew in a quick breath through my teeth. My body was filled with pleasure once again. Jacob began pounding me hard, pulling me toward him firmly while at the same time bucking his hips forward. He had total control and I loved it. Everything about it felt incredible.

Wave after wave of ecstasy crashed over me, causing my limbs to go weak. I couldn't hold myself up, so I dropped down, letting the upper part of my body collapse into the comforter. I was trembling, as every inch of my skin exploded with sensation. Each thrust of his cock sent another wave, pushing me toward a climax that I had been waiting so long to enjoy.

After a few seconds, I managed to push myself back up with my arms. My breasts swayed now, nipples dragging over the top of the bed with each movement. I couldn't remember a time when I had felt that much pleasure all at once, and it was enough to send me over the top.

I climaxed hard as sensation overwhelmed me. I drew in a breath and began to exhale. Only a soft squeal went past my lips as I rode the orgasm all the way to the top, where I enjoyed the most mind-numbing bliss I had ever experienced.

I wish it could have lasted forever. My legs trembled as the sensation slowly tapered off and the intensity faded. By the time I could remind myself to breathe again, I had relaxed my head back down on the bed.

Jacob continued, though, pounding me harder than before. He gripped both hips and pulled me toward him so firmly that my knees lifted up from the bed. After a moment, I turned to look over my shoulder. He looked as beautiful as ever, with a light layer of sweat covering his skin and a determined expression on his face.

"Come for me," I said.

He glanced up and nodded, increasing the pace of his thrusts even further.

I loved watching him take me like that. I enjoyed the feeling of his hands on my hips and the strength of his thrusts. It made me feel small and vulnerable in front of him, and somehow that made him appear even sexier.

It didn't take long. He held his fast pace for a few minutes and then I watched his cheeks flush. With one final plunge, he pulled me toward him and held himself inside of me. I loved the way he filled me, the way my body reacted to his in such a primal way.

It took Jacob a few moments to collect himself, but when he did, he crawled up next to me on the bed. I laid my head onto his chest. I could hear his heartbeat, still rapid after his orgasm.

"That just made these last six weeks totally worth it," I said, with a smirk.

Jacob kissed the top of my head and squeezed my shoulder.

"I just don't ever want to have to wait six weeks again," he groaned. "I know anticipation is good, but it nearly killed me."

Using my index finger, I began to draw imaginary lines over Jacob's pecks. I circled his nipples, then moved down toward his abs. I bounced over them, all the way to the line of his hips, before making my way back up.

"We won't wait six weeks again," I said. "I promise."

I had hardly finished my sentence before I heard some movement on the other side of my bedroom door. It was the sound of pots and pans clanging in the kitchen, and I knew instantly that Lauren was home. I blushed and sat up, looking at Jacob.

"Do you think she heard us?" I asked, instantly feeling embarrassed.

Jacob simply shrugged and his lips curled up into a devilish smile. "Maybe. Is it weird that I kind of hope she did?"

"You haven't even met her yet," I said, playfully slapping him on the shoulder. "She will have heard us having sex before even seeing your face."

Jacob sat up and kissed my cheek, before laying back

down. He placed his hands behind his head as he looked up at the ceiling, in a relaxed pose.

"That's one hell of an introduction," he said, with a laugh.

"Very funny," I said, as I poked his stomach.

Then I laid back down and snuggled next to him once again. I felt so content laying there next to Jacob. I realized then how important he was to my well being and how I never wanted there to be a time that I'd have to lay in that bed alone ever again.

"You're staying with me tonight, right?" I asked, snuggling contentedly into his shoulder.

"I actually have a hotel," he replied. My heart sank.

"Oh." My throat tightened and I wondered if we were going to see each other at all this weekend.

"I was rather hoping you would join me," he said, kissing my forehead. "Since you have your roommate here, I thought we would be more comfortable by ourselves."

My heart turned from lead to helium. "Of course! I would love to!"

He chuckled and nuzzled me with his nose. "You want to go now? That way you can be loud next time."

"Give me three minutes to pack my bags," I told him, already jumping out of bed.

CHAPTER 16

"Are you feeling any better?" Jacob asked, coming over and kissing my forehead. I was still wrapped up in the soft hotel bedding after dragging myself from the bathroom. I smiled and leaned into his kiss, enjoying the tender caress.

"Much," I promised. "I just hope I don't give you whatever stomach bug I've got."

Jacob sat on the edge of the bed. "It would be worth it," he assured me. "Besides, I've got a cast-iron stomach. Nothing gets me."

I hoped he was right. I had woken up first thing in the morning to yet again loose my dinner. Jacob had ordered room service, but all I had managed to eat was a piece of toast and some orange juice. The juice had actually tasted better than the coffee, which again, I had only been able to get a couple of swallows down.

"At least I don't have to clean the bathroom here," I joked. Jacob laughed.

"I will get you a hotel room any time you are sick," he promised. "Or a maid."

"You spoil me," I replied with a smile. He grinned.

"That's part of how I plan to keep you," he said, brushing a lock of hair from my face.

"You're doing a great job so far," I told him, glancing around the room. I still had no idea how Jacob had swung this room. It was the fanciest, most amazing hotel room I had ever seen.

The room was bigger than my current apartment and the shower alone was as big as my bedroom. We had an ocean-facing room with had huge windows with electric shades that hid the floor to ceiling windows with a touch of a button. Currently, I was laying in a giant white bed watching boats bob on the ocean. It was amazing.

I had no idea how Jacob had managed to get such a nice room, and I didn't want to know what he was paying for it. He promised me that he could afford it and that it was meant to make sure we both had a wonderful, relaxing weekend.

"What do they want?" I asked Jacob as he looked at his phone and sighed for the third time in ten minutes.

"Who?" He pocketed his phone and gave me a fake smile.

I raised my eyebrows and waited.

"It's HR for my company," he said, relenting. He pushed his glasses up on his nose. "They heard I was in town, and they want me to come in and do some paperwork. Apparently, I'm behind on health insurance benefits or something."

I thought about it for a moment. I was feeling better, but I wasn't ready to leave this bed yet. My stomach was still queasy and I was still low on energy after my six-weeks of no sleep.

"Go," I told him. "I'll stay here and catch up on some emails and sleep."

Jacob looked surprised. "Really?"

"All I want to do right now is sleep, and you're already up and dressed." I shrugged. "Go sign your paperwork and when you get back, I'll be ready to be active. Or go back to bed." I gave him a seductive wink.

"You naughty girl," he said with a grin.

"Oh, you have no idea. I have plans for this evening that will make naughty your favorite word," I promised, thinking of the special underwear I had tucked into my suitcase.

I loved the way his eyes dilated and the grin that spread across his face.

"Then I will make this a quick trip," he told me as he stood up. I watched as he grabbed his computer bag and gave me a quick kiss before heading out the door.

When he was gone, I snuggled deeper into the luxurious white bedspread and tried to close my eyes, but even though I was exhausted, sleep wouldn't come. My body was relaxed and ready to sleep, but my eyes just wouldn't stay closed.

With a sigh, I went and retrieved my laptop and brought it back to bed with me. Moving took more energy than I really had to give, but I wanted my computer. If nothing else, now was a good time to look over my job offer. I still had the rest of today and all of tomorrow to decide if I wanted the job on Monday.

I opened up my email and downloaded the attachment. I could feel my forehead crinkle as I read down the list of job expectations and my eyebrows raised.

Some of the expectations, like working overtime and restricted social media, didn't surprise me after my internship. The company was extremely fast-paced and pushed their employees to go as far as they could.

But, the expectations of living within ten miles, being available by cell phone at all times even on days off, strict travel restrictions, and working weekends were more than I was ready for. The attachment was over four pages of social limitations and how much time I needed to spend at the office.

As I scrolled through the document, I realized that the job was basically an extension of the internship. It was just more ridiculously long hours and unending loyalty to the company, but for a lot more money.

The only thing that made me even pause on closing the entire computer was the salary at the bottom. Even at Silicon Valley prices, it was an impressive paycheck. I would be making more than I could dream of asking as a recently graduated programmer. I could afford a house. I could afford a lot of things with that salary.

I chewed on my lip, trying to decide just how bad the last six weeks had been. They had been rough. Super rough. But, a paycheck like that would allow me a lot of freedom to do other things.

A new email popped up on my computer and I flipped over to it. It was from the computer company that Lauren worked for. She had mentioned me to her boss, and now there was a job interview if I wanted it. When they said that winning this internship opened up doors, they weren't kidding.

I clicked on the offer and looked through it. The job was similar to what Lauren was doing now, but the pay was nowhere near what ZephTech was offering. However, the hours were way better and there was no talk of mandatory overtime or living proximity requirements.

A job with great hours, or a job with great pay? I was leaning toward a job with great pay until I thought of Jacob.

Even if I was making a million dollars a month, if I didn't have a chance to see him, I would hate my job. If I couldn't spend any of that money on going out to see him or renting a hotel like this, the money the job gave me wouldn't be worth it.

"I can't believe I'm not going to take it," I whispered to the empty room. It was so strange to consider. I had worked my whole college career for this job, but now that it was here, I didn't want it. At least not the way they were going to give it to me.

I wanted a life. Not a job. The job wasn't my end-all be-all any more. I wanted more than just a cool title and a big salary. I realized I would be far happier with a job like Lauren's where I could go home and see Jacob whenever I wanted than having to work all the time and be rich.

I opened an email to draft my response to ZephTech. And then I sat there, staring at the empty document. I couldn't think of the words to write. I knew that I would need to inform them of my decision, yet I was having difficulty actually saying that this was no longer my dream.

My phone chimed and there was a text from Jacob.

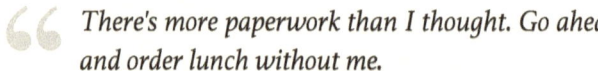

There's more paperwork than I thought. Go ahead and order lunch without me.

I LET OUT A SHARP BREATH. Food was still the last thing on my mind. Except maybe some more orange juice. That sounded good.

I closed the message and was about to set my phone down when I saw the icon for the Monster GO game. I hadn't played since my internship had started since I didn't have time for anything else.

I had heard that playing it in bigger cities was more fun as there were more people and things to do, so I started it up. It would at least be something to do to clear my head while I figured out how to turn down the job I had worked so hard to get.

There were several updates that needed to be approved and I wondered just how many new features to the game had been added since I had last played. It only took a moment. I scrolled down the list, feeling an odd sense of deja vu.

There was now the ability to battle individuals, a friends list, a nearby players list, custom monster tracking, gym notifications, friend notifications, and custom monster lures. I frowned slightly as I went through them. Those were all things that I had thought of to make the game better months ago when I had been playing.

"Wow, I was really on trend for this," I said out loud. A bit of smug pride filled me and I considered texting Jacob to tell him my latest discovery. I had been right on the money for what the game needed. If only I could find a way to make a job out of that I would be set.

I played the game for a few minutes. The difference between playing at home and playing in a big city was night and day. I didn't even have to leave my bed to access a Monster Stop here, whereas at home I had to walk three blocks. Just due to the increased population density, I caught three monsters just in my hotel room.

Tommy would be so jealous.

I considered getting up and going for a walk. There was so much more to do in the game here than back home that I was really tempted. Except the bed was so comfortable and walking sounded like too much work.

When I had exhausted what I could do in the game from my hotel bed, I turned off the game and checked my email one more time. All that was there was a news alert. I had set up an alert to let me know if anything new came up about the Monster Go Billionaire App creator. Apparently, just in the last hour, three news sites had mentioned him. I thought back to the numerous articles I'd come across while browsing twitter and the many Monster GO pieces, all of which referenced a creator that had fled Silicon Valley.

I clicked on the link and froze.

It wasn't the headline that was inducing sweat at the top of my forehead. It was the picture.

I reread the headline for a second time as my heart dropped into my stomach; "*App Developer Back From Hiding*" it said.

Below the headline was a picture of Jacob looking candidly into the distance.

CHAPTER 17

J sat in shock as I stared at the picture. It was most definitely Jacob. He was wearing the shirt he had left in and had the dark rimmed glasses that I thought made him look so smart on.

Slowly, I read the first article:

> *Reclusive Monster GO billionaire, Jacob Rigby, seen here exiting his new headquarters in Silicon Valley. After the sudden success of the game, the developer disappeared from Silicon Valley to regroup. Little to no information of the developer was available at that time.*
>
> *Fans were afraid that without the designer at the helm, the game would stagnate. But, during the last six weeks, major game changes were put into play and offices were opened as the company went on a hiring spree. Mr. Rigby has been incredibly busy with his business.*
>
> *Whatever Mr. Rigby did to regroup has*

worked well as the new updates to the game have
fans joining in the highest numbers yet. The battle
feature as well as the ability to see nearby friends
has been lauded as "incredible" and "brilliant."

Seen here, Rigby is leaving his new
headquarters in Silicon Valley. This is the first
time he has been seen in person at this location.

I COULDN'T BELIEVE what I was reading. Apparently Jacob had used my absence to work on his business using my ideas. I knew now why the features had seemed familiar. It was because I had come up with them during a walk with Jacob. He had jokingly asked if he should be writing them down, but now I wondered if he had actually done just that.

No wonder he didn't want to come to Silicon Valley. He didn't want to be caught like he just was. He was hiding out in my home town because he was too chicken to work on his own game.

I re-read the article, getting angrier and more heated by every word. "The ability to battle and see nearby friends was incredible and brilliant?" He was getting credit for my ideas.

Not to mention the part of the article that mentioned his game company had just gone on a major hiring spree. I guess it was easy to just steal his girlfriend's ideas rather than pay her. Why give her a job when she does it all for free? Just make sure she's too busy to notice what you're doing.

Only now, I was noticing. All the little things that should have given it away. Anger swelled in my chest. The Legazeus wasn't just a random occurrence. He had put it there for our picnic. The updates that were always my ideas, the Monster

Stop on the way to my house- it was all him. It was all him using me to improve his game.

He didn't care about me. It was cheaper to date me than it was to hire me.

Hot, angry tears trickled down my face and I wiped them away so hard it hurt. How dare he do this to me. How stupid did he think I was? Did he think I wouldn't figure it out?

There was no way I wasn't taking the ZephTech job now. There was no reason not to. I wasn't with Jacob anymore. I couldn't be with Jacob anymore.

I threw the bed sheets off and slammed my feet on the floor. I didn't think as I threw all my things back in my suitcase and got dressed. There was no way I was staying the rest of the weekend here. There was no way I was staying with him.

I pulled up a car-driving app and requested a driver to take me home immediately.

I had no idea when Jacob was supposed to be back, but I wanted to make sure he knew why I had left, so I grabbed my lipstick out of my bag and went to the mirror.

MONSTER GO IS A LIE, I wrote in big red letters. I hated how dumb it sounded after I wrote it, but I wasn't about to wash it off. I added, FUCK YOU underneath, just to make sure he was clear on my feelings.

I'd never felt so used. So lied to.

I could have forgiven him for not telling me who he was. I would have been angry, but I probably could have come around to it if he had told me himself.

But he didn't. A news story had told me.

It was the fact that he had used all my ideas and was taking the credit for them that had me so angry. I had worked my butt off to the point of being ill for this stupid internship, and all it would have taken was a wave of his hand to hire me. Instead, he let me sweat and toil while he took the glory.

I loved him and he had used me without so much as a thank you. No wonder he could afford such a nice hotel. He certainly wasn't using his earnings to pay me for my ideas.

I grabbed all my belongings and stormed out the door. The heavy hotel door gave a satisfying shake to the hallway when I slammed it.

I was halfway across the hotel lobby when I heard him call my name.

"Alicia?"

I stopped, turning to see Jacob walking up the marble entrance with a stupid look on his face. My vision went red.

"Leave me alone," I growled, trying to get around him. If I wasn't so furious by his betrayal, I might have actually cared about the hurt look that filled his face. "It's over."

"What? What are you talking about?" He stood there as if he didn't have a clue, but he wouldn't let me pass either.

"Billionaire Monster GO developer, huh?" I held up my phone with the news article. "Interesting job description, Jacob."

His mouth opened and he paled. "Alicia, I can explain..."

"You can explain?" My voice rose to almost supersonic levels. "You can explain how you used all my ideas without saying a word? How you hired hundreds of people, but not me? How you kept it all a secret?"

He winced as though I hit him with every word. "Alicia, please-"

"No, no 'Alicia please.'" I shouldered past him. "You *used* me. You *lied* to me. You lied to *everyone*. I hate you."

Jacob stilled as I screamed that last sentence across the

hotel lobby. Everyone turned and looked, but I didn't care. I was too angry, too hurt to care.

He reached out to touch my arm and I snarled and batted it away. "Don't you dare touch me."

"Alicia..."

"Leave me alone, Jacob. I don't want anything to do with you." I stormed past him to get in my waiting car. "You can get some other stupid girl to make your game for you."

He winced and stepped back as if I had actually pushed him. I wished I could have beaten him with my fist. I just wanted to go home. I just wanted to wake up and find that this was a terrible dream.

But I knew it wasn't.

The man I loved was a lie. He didn't love me. He loved my game ideas, not me.

I managed to keep a strong face until I got in the car. The driver made it all the way to the end of the block before I burst out in tears and cried the rest of the way home.

CHAPTER 18

*M*onday morning came, and it took everything to crawl out of bed. My whole body hurt with heartache and all I wanted to do was sleep until I didn't need to cry anymore. It wasn't the way I had envisioned starting my dream job at ZephTech, but then nothing about the past three days had gone as I'd expected.

I blinked several times before standing up. My stomach was still lurching back and forth. Whatever stomach bug I had was still with me. The act of standing hadn't helped any, but I ignored it as best I could as I lumbered into the shower.

The air was fiercely cold against my wet skin when I stepped out, a feeling that gave new energy to the wrench in my stomach. I took several deep breaths while I leaned over the toilet, hoping to prevent myself from falling back into a spiral of vomiting. Finally, I zombie-walked back into my room, the shower not having done anything to cure my exhaustion.

The lit up digits on the clock beside my bed suddenly

caught my attention like fireworks in the sky; it was 8:45 AM, fifteen minutes before I was supposed to be at work.

I must've showered for longer than I thought. I threw my hair in a messy bun and scrambled to assemble an appropriate outfit. My dress paints were still sitting where I'd tossed them after work last Friday and I quickly threw them on, deciding no one would notice such a subtle detail.

It was 8:58 AM when I pulled into a spot at the edge of the ZephTech building parking lot, a rather miraculous accomplishment. This was my first day not arriving at least ten—usually fifteen—minutes early. *Not a good look for your first day on the job*, I thought. But considering that I was still wet and fighting off nausea fifteen minutes prior to *today's* workday, this was probably the best I could've hoped for.

I hurried over to where the interns would meet every morning. No one was there now since I was the only surviving intern left. I sat down and waited for my boss.

"Mornin' Alicia," Steve Lynchell said, walking over to me. He was tall with short blond hair dark enough that it looked almost brown in the right lighting.

"Good morning, Mr. Lynchell," I said, willing a smile onto my face despite the churn in my stomach. I couldn't believe I still didn't feel good.

"Come on, call me Steve," he said. "I know you can do it."

I giggled awkwardly.

He chuckled too. "Go on, give it a try."

"Good morning, Steve," I said.

"There you go. Much better." He smiled at me. "You're not an intern anymore."

"I know," I said, not really knowing how else to reply.

"You're a permanent member of our team now," he said.

"It's good to be on the team," I said. "*Great* to be on the team, actually."

"Good, I'm glad to hear that," Steve Lynchell said. "Welcome to your first *real* day with ZephTech." He did a sweeping sort of motion with his hand as he spoke.

"Thank you," I said, and for a brief second my forced smile found a bit of authenticity.

"Head on over to my secretary's desk," he told me. "She'll get you to fill out the necessary paperwork and she'll show you where your desk is. Welcome officially aboard."

"Thank you, sir," I replied. He frowned slightly. "I mean, thank you, *Steve*."

He smiled and patted my shoulder before turning and making his way through the office to greet the rest of his employees. I felt another spout of nausea and fought it down, not wanting to run to the bathroom.

Everyone would probably think I'm hung over or something, I thought. And I couldn't have that, especially not on my first day.

I wanted to work with the sort of energy and enthusiasm that *should've* been there on my first day, but instead I was inescapably tired. Whatever virus I had was zapping my energy.

The day went on without incident. I managed to sign everything and find my new desk. It was the same as the desk I had used for my internship, just next to a window. That was the only difference I could find. Other than that, everything felt the same.

There was the same nervous energy, the same constant threat that I needed to perform my best, and the same look of disapproval from other staff when I yawned. Other than the fact that I my paycheck was going to be much bigger, my life was the same it had been two weeks ago.

Well, without Jacob, I amended to myself. And for the first time that day, I was glad I was going to be so busy. I didn't want to think about him. I didn't want to think about the fact that I was here because he was a total dick.

I looked around. The view from my window was just of another building, but it was better than nothing. I could make a future here. I hoped.

I opened up my email and found a mountain of work already awaiting me. My internship was over and the work-load was just as intense. It loomed over me now, since there was no end-date. I buckled down. I didn't really have a life outside of this now anyway.

The day flew by. I worked and kept my head down, eating a light lunch that I managed to keep down, but by dinner I was done. It was even more work than when I was an intern. I was exhausted and needed to go home. I stood up and stretched, gathered my things, and left.

All my co-workers watched as I left. Even though it was well after six, I was the first one out of the office.

So much for making a good first day, I thought, barely keeping down a yawn. I managed to find my car and start driving home, only to hit the end of rush-hour traffic. At least it was mindless to sit in traffic.

I looked around, watching people singing in their cars or talking on the phone. For a moment, I wished I had someone to talk to. But I stuffed that ache down fast. If I wanted to talk to someone, I could talk to Caroline. Or my mom. I didn't need to talk to *him*.

The car crept forward. There was a giant billboard advertisement for baby wipes, with a beautiful newborn gazing directly into my soul and telling me to buy those specific wipes.

The baby's eyes were blue. Like Jacob's.

I couldn't stop the tears from starting. It had been a rough day and now I was thinking about how I would never have children with Jacob. Three days ago, I had been sure that we were meant to be together forever and that our future was rosy and bright. I had already imagined marrying him and having babies just like the one on that sign.

Only, it wasn't going to happen. It never was, to be honest, but now I knew it.

I was crying so hard, I could barely see straight. I wasn't fit to drive, so I took the next exit and pulled into the parking lot of a grocery store and proceeded to bawl my eyes out for the next fifteen minutes.

The sun had set by the time I finally pulled myself together. I didn't really feel any better, but now I was empty. I didn't have any more energy to cry. I was hollow.

My stomach rumbled and for the first time all day, I felt hungry. Orange juice again sounded like nectar of the gods, and luckily I was parked in front of a grocery store.

I wiped my face, grimacing in the rear-view mirror as I tried to look socially acceptable. I hoped people wouldn't look too closely, because I was a mess. My wet-dried hair was all over the place, my suit was wrinkled and I had spilled something on it, and now my face was splotchy and I no longer had any eye makeup on.

I looked like I had just been dumped, so at least I matched how I felt.

The neon lights of the store hummed as I picked up a basket and avoided any social contact. I ran from the nice woman in a red shirt who was putting canned goods away, not wanting to even make eye-contact with another human being.

Slowly, I walked the aisles, picking out things that

sounded good. Orange juice, pickles, ice cream, and salt-n-vinegar chips all went in my basket.

"What, are you pregnant?" I asked myself as I tossed in a bag of gummy bears that suddenly looked delicious. I meant it as a joke, but it made me freeze.

Ice cream and pickles?

I couldn't remember what day it was. I nearly dropped my basket of food as I scrambled for my phone, desperate to check the date.

I was late. *Way* late.

"No way," I said out loud. "There's no way."

Subconsciously my hands gravitated to my stomach and I dropped them as soon as I realized.

No. I'm on birth control, I thought. It was the same reason I hadn't been concerned over a missed period, with them coming every three months it'd be another three or four weeks before I was even due. *Birth control,* I repeated to myself, now hearing my own voice in my head. *It's never failed before. All four years of college it never failed.*

I swallowed hard, trying to fight off panic. I couldn't remember the last time I'd taken my birth control, which shouldn't have been a problem since I wasn't having sex during my internship. Except, I couldn't remember the last time I'd taken it from before my internship.

"Okay," I said out loud again, finding a weird comfort in lecturing myself. Luckily, the store was mostly deserted. "Time to buy a test."

At the very least I needed to rule it out, I decided. Then, at that point I could go to a doctor and get some antibiotics or whatever I needed to fight the infection I'd caught. It had to be some sort of infection and my immune system was just causing me to crave weird things.

I walked quickly over to the feminine needs aisle. I appreciated the irony of pregnancy tests being next to the condoms and within spitting distance of the tampons. If you needed one of these things, you didn't need the other.

My hands shook as I selected two boxes. One was far cheaper than the other, but the more expensive box promised an easy digital readout. I wanted to be absolutely sure.

"I'm making the big bucks now," I whispered, putting the more expensive one in my basket. "And digital is what got me into this mess. Maybe it will get me out."

I glanced through my basket and realized I didn't need anything else. Except maybe more orange juice, I wanted gallons of that, so I began the walk to the checkout. With every step, I was sure people were watching me. I felt the security cameras on my every move as I put my things on the counter to buy. I did my best not to cringe as I put the pregnancy test up there.

I was sweating when the clerk swiped the test. I was ready with an "it's for a friend!" response if she said anything. But she didn't. She just scanned it and put it in a bag with my three gallons of orange juice.

"Have a great day," the cashier told me as she handed me the bag. I expected judgment, but instead there was just a world-weary smile. I wondered just how many women she saw buy pregnancy tests on a daily basis.

I considered going to the bathroom of the grocery store, but chickened out. I told myself if was because I had ice cream that would melt if I didn't get it in the freezer, but I knew that wasn't the real reason. The last place I wanted to find out if I was pregnant or not was the grocery store because I wasn't sure how I was going to react.

I already looked like a crazy person with my three gallons of orange juice, tear streaked face, and psychotic hair. I didn't need to come out of the bathroom screaming, so I just went home.

CHAPTER 19

I peed on the stick.
And waited.

And waited.

And waited.

It felt like an eternity. I paced the bathroom, I sat on the toilet, I straightened up my shower toiletries, yet the time did not pass. It was the longest five minutes of my life.

My hands shook as I approached the sink. It was the moment of truth. I was half afraid the test would somehow be inconclusive, despite the box's assurances that wouldn't happen.

I swallowed hard and picked up the test.

PREGNANT

IT WAS WRITTEN THERE in big bold letters.

I shook it, just to be sure.

PREGNANT

I DIDN'T KNOW if I should scream, cry, pass out or laugh. I felt like I should probably do all of the above. I wished I had someone here to hold my hand as I read that dark word that meant my life was changing. I wished I had Jacob, the one who didn't lie to me, with me telling me that everything was going to be okay and that this was a blessing.

I wished I had someone who would help me tell my dad.

I sank slowly onto the toilet and felt a tear trickle down my cheek as I pressed my hand against my stomach.

I already loved the life growing inside of me. Now that I knew it was there, I loved it. It didn't matter that its father was a lying bastard. It didn't matter that it changed everything and I wasn't sure what I was going to do about that yet.

I loved that life and was determined to do whatever it took to keep it healthy.

My phone buzzed on the counter and I looked over to see a message from Jacob. I immediately deleted it as I didn't care what he had to say to me. I was still furious and wanted nothing to do with him and his apologies.

Do I have to tell him? I asked myself. *Does he even deserve to know?*

I looked at the positive test and knew that I should. I didn't have a clue how, though. It was the right thing to do, even if it would be terrible. I stood up and washed my hands.

"Oh, hi Jacob. I know that you're a lying POS, but you now have a baby," I said cheerfully to the mirror. "Yeah, that's going to go over well."

I ran my fingers through my hair, trying to think. How in the world was I going to tell him? The last person on the entire planet I wanted to talk to was now the person I had to tell something very important to and I didn't know how to do it.

"I can't tell him right now," I whispered. Not after that fight. I still didn't even want to think his name, let alone think of having a conversation. It just wasn't something I was ready to do.

"I'll tell him after it's confirmed by the doctor," I told the mirror. Mirror me did not look impressed.

I would call the doctor in the morning and set up an appointment. After that, I would tell Jacob. I knew that there was still a possibility that this was a false pregnancy, or that I could lose the baby, so I didn't want to tell him too early.

"You just don't want to tell him at all, and you're using that as an excuse," Mirror me said. I stuck my tongue out at her. Still, I needed a little bit of time and waiting for the official word from the doctor seemed like it was the best idea.

I took a deep breath and tried not to panic.

"You okay in there?" Lauren called through the door.

"Fine," I lied. "Just finishing up."

"Okay, I just need to take a shower before bed," Lauren replied. I listened to her footsteps head off into her room.

I snapped a picture of the pregnancy test on my phone and then wrapped it in toilet paper and tossed it in the trash. I thought about leaving it, but the idea that somehow Lauren would find it made me too nervous. I grabbed the bag and took it to the outside garbage.

The night sky was peaceful as I walked to the communal garbage. In the distance a dog barked and I could hear a jet plane overhead, but overall, it was a quiet and soothing night. I looked up at the sky, wishing I could see just a few more stars to make a wish on.

I had wished on stars for my job at ZephTech, and that

had come true. Maybe, I could wish for everything to turn out right and that would happen too.

I paused, sending up a grateful thank you to the stars for giving me my job at ZephTech. For the first time since accepting the position, I was glad. The salary would be enough to support me and the baby, and as a full-time employee I had excellent health insurance. Because of the job, I wouldn't have to ask Jacob to help with the baby.

I smiled at the stars. The universe was telling me that I had made the right decision. It was putting me where I needed to be. Things were going to work out the way they were supposed to.

I was going to make it. I was proud of myself. I didn't need his help or his love. I was strong enough to do this.

Granted, Jacob could pay for a dozen nannies and a private hospital since he was apparently a billionaire, but I didn't want to ask him for a cent. I wanted nothing to do with him, even if it would make my life easier.

He can spend his money on the baby, I told myself. *I don't want any of his dirty money.*

I pushed away the small voice saying that it would be easier to do this with him. That I still loved him. I pushed away the voice that asked if I really could do this. The job was so demanding that I was barely making it while pregnant and I wasn't sure what I would do once the child was born.

One step at a time, I told myself. One step at a time.

I would keep my job until something better came along. Once the baby was born, I could move back home and ask my parents for help. I could work from home and I would have the support of my family. Until then, I would just save as much of my giant paycheck as I possibly could.

It felt good to have a plan.

Bing.

A new email popped up on my phone. The subject line was about a new job opportunity. At first, my instinct was to ignore the email. Now that I had won the ZephTech internship, I was receiving job interviews that would have made me scream for joy seven weeks ago. But, there was something about this one that caught my eye. I recognized the company as one that made some of my favorite games.

 Dear Alicia Chambers,

As the winner of the ZephTech internship, we would like to invite you to interview for a brand new position at our new off shoot company, DragonFury Gaming.

We've seen great success in the past year and are in need of a new development programmer. We believe that your creative skills and passion for programming would be the perfect fit for our company.

The details of the position are below. Please call to schedule an interview.

I QUICKLY SCANNED the email and my breath caught. It was a game development company that was branching off of one of my favorite gaming systems. I could barely believe my eyes. The more I read, the more it sounded like what I wanted the ZephTech position to be.

I read it three times just to be sure. I'd been fooled into thinking that a job was exactly what I wanted once before, and I wasn't in a hurry to do so again. Yet, what harm could a job interview do? I didn't have to take the new position, but it might be a better fit than what I currently had at ZephTech.

I put the phone back in my pocket and looked up once more at the sky. The universe really was looking out for this baby, I decided and I went back inside.

CHAPTER 20

*I*t was now Friday at three, and I was ready for my interview. I'd barely been at ZephTech as a full time employee for a week now, and I was ready to pull my hair out. I hated it. Without having an end date, every day was worse than before. My heart just wasn't in doing every-thing for the company with only a pat on the back for reward. I was looking forward to this job interview. I was hoping it would give me something a little less demanding, something that I could continue to do once the baby was born. Even if it didn't pan out, I was excited for the job inter-view as a chance to expand my horizons.

I wore my best suit. It was a dark gray with strong lines that I felt projected strength and dependability. At least, I hoped it did. Paired with some cute low pumps, I felt ready to take on the world.

My phone buzzed. It was another phone call from Jacob. I didn't answer it. I still didn't want to talk to him. I'd told Lauren that he wasn't allowed in the apartment, and upon hearing that he had used my programming ideas, she was furious. She had actually gone out in the hallway the one time he had tried to see me and she told him off herself.

After the cops were called by some worried neighbors, he stopped trying to come to the apartment. I was just glad his emails, texts, and calls were easy to delete, even if every one of them reminded me that I needed to tell him about the baby eventually. But, the key word in that sentence was *eventually*.

I parked my car and made sure my resume was still tucked neatly in a folder along with some samples of my work. I was ready for my interview.

Thankfully, my morning sickness was behaving itself. Since figuring out that was the culprit, I had changed my eating habits. I had ginger ale on me at all times and made sure that I had saltine crackers to keep something in my stomach. It wasn't exactly a cure, but it did seem to help.

I parked my car and started walking to the interview location. We were to meet at a chess table in the middle of a large park nearby and I was given exact GPS coordinates. I was rather surprised that it was outdoors, but the woman on the phone said that the boss liked to be a little informal for job interviews. He felt that putting people in nature tended to show their true qualities, or something like that.

Either way, it was going to be a unique interview.

I easily found the chess table and took a seat, making sure that I looked put together and ready for my interview. I was a couple of minutes early, so I double checked that I was in the right location. According to my GPS, I was exactly where I was supposed to be.

I took a deep breath and rehearsed my job interview questions in my head. I was half way through telling myself of a time when I went above and beyond on a project when I noticed someone walking toward me. It was a younger man in comfortable clothing, but considering anything went in the tech world, I wasn't terribly surprised. I stood up and smiled, ready to greet my prospective future employer.

"Mr. Brandish?" I asked, holding out my hand. "Peter Brandish?"

The man looked up from his phone and shook his head. "No, I'm here for the monster."

I stared at him for a good two seconds before he motioned to the table behind me. "What?"

"Oh, I see it," he replied, pointing to my table. He held up his phone and spoke into the speaker. "I'm Sorry Alicia."

I continued to stare at him like he was speaking in tongues, but he wasn't paying attention to me now anyway. He moved his finger across the screen and grinned before walking away.

I wasn't quite sure what to do, so I just sat back down at the table.

"Excuse me," a young woman said, coming up to me. She held up her phone and spoke into it. "I'm Sorry Alicia."

"What?" I asked, not sure I had heard her correctly. "How do you know my name?"

"I don't," the woman replied as she grinned at her phone. "But it's how you catch the monster."

"The monster?" I was so confused, but the woman was gone. More people had come up to my area and were speaking into their phones. A murmur of "I'm Sorry Alicia" was filling the air as more and more people came and said it.

"What in the hell is going on?" I asked completely confused.

The question was really to myself, but a young boy heard me and responded. "We're here for the I'm Sorry Alicia. It one of the rarest Monsters that the game has introduced. Nobody has even heard of it before today."

"The I'm Sorry Alicia?" I asked. "What the hell is that?"

But the boy was gone, replaced with another person speaking the words and attempting to catch the creature.

Within seconds, the entire park was filled with people. They were all holding their phones, cramming up against my chess table. They all kept saying, "I'm Sorry Alicia," into their phones and then grinning before walking away.

"I don't know any of you!" I shouted.

"We don't know you either," one responded. She looked like an aging soccer mom. She wore the same smirk of excitement as the rest of the people surrounding her.

"Then how do you all know my name?" I asked.

"We don't," the lady said. "We just want to catch the I'm Sorry Alicia. The only way to catch it is to say 'I'm sorry, Alicia' into the mouthpiece. As soon as you do that, you get a special ball that can catch it."

A Monster? Like from the game? I thought. I was about to ask her more, but the woman was gone.

I reached my hand down into my pocket to grab my cell phone. The crowd pushed past me, nearly knocking me over as they did so. I managed to stay standing as I opened up the Monster GO app on my phone.

Sure enough, there was a Monster nearby. It was named "I'm Sorry Alicia." I held my phone up to see the digital Monster standing on the chess table. It was drawn in the style of the other monsters, but it was obviously based on Jacob and me. Technically, it was two monsters, one male with blue fur and the other female with beautiful curly hair. Their hands were entwined, making them a single creature.

Underneath, the information bar said they were lovers that were meant to be together. Separating them caused great harm.

My mind was filled with confusion. A hand on my

shoulder caused me to look up and when I saw who it was, I nearly dropped the phone.

"Jacob," I whispered.

"Hey, gorgeous," he replied.

My heart stalled. He was so damn handsome. I had missed him so much this week, but I was still incredibly pissed at him. I wanted to hug him and slug him right in the throat at the same time.

"You need to make these people leave," I told him, raising my voice over the murmurs of "I'm Sorry Alicia." I needed to stay strong. "I have a job interview..."

He gave me a small, wry smile.

"*You're* the interview, aren't you?" I asked, feeling incredibly annoyed as I figured it out. "It's how you knew I'd be here."

Jacob at least had the grace to look slightly abashed. "Peter Brandish is my uncle."

I felt my hand curl up into a ball, and I wanted to hit something. I had been so excited for this interview. It had been everything I wanted in a job and now I learned that I had just taken time off from my real job for something that didn't exist.

"How dare you," I hissed, though I wasn't sure he could hear me over the players still saying 'I'm Sorry Alicia.' "You knew exactly what would get me here."

He frowned, his blue eyes desperate behind his glasses. "It was the only way I could think of to get you to talk to me."

I turned to leave, but there was a wall of people blocking my way. The noise from all the people saying "I'm Sorry Alicia" was nearly deafening.

"I can't believe you would do this," I yelled, turning back

to him. Tears caught in my throat. "How could you do this to me?"

Jacob frowned and tapped something into his phone. This clearly wasn't going the way he had expected it to.

"It's gone," he announced to the crowd. A collected moan of disappointment rippled through the crowd. I glanced down to see that the monster was gone from my phone screen. There was nothing there to even hint that anything had happened.

As quickly as the crowd had accumulated, it disappeared.

"Why the hell would you do this?" I asked him once it was quiet enough to talk again.

"Because you wouldn't talk to me," he replied. "That's all I want. Just to explain myself."

I scoffed. "Go for it. I'm not sure how you plan on explaining what you did, but you are welcome to try. Apparently, I have an hour that's no longer booked."

He motioned to the chess table and we both sat.

"I never meant to hurt you," he started.

"Of course you didn't," I sneered. "You just meant to use me."

He looked down, his shoulders slumping. "No, I never meant to use you."

I crossed my arms and leaned back. "Then why the hell did you do it? Why did you lie to me and use my ideas? Why would you do that?"

He took a shaky breath in. "I didn't tell you I was a billionaire because I wanted you to want *me*, not my money. The money has been so overwhelming, that it was the best thing in the world to find someone who didn't know."

"You slept with me," I said, narrowing my eyes. "You let

me hunt for a job while you ran a billion dollar corporation and could have given me a job in a second."

"Because you would have wanted to earn it," he shot back. He took a breath and pulled off his glasses, folding them in his hands. "You wanted to earn that job at ZephTech."

"So? I would have taken a job from you," I told him. "I would have taken a job."

"I used your ideas so you could see how perfect they were." He folded and unfolded his glasses, saying his words calmly. "My plan was to show you how successful your ideas were, how perfect you were for the job. Then you would have known that I didn't just give it to you, that it was your job by rights. Not by gift."

A crack in my hardened heart appeared. I couldn't help it.

"I told my team that the updates were from a bright new designer, not from me," he continued. "You earned the job I was going to offer you."

"Then why didn't you offer it?" I asked, tightening my crossed arms.

"I was going to have you come to the office on Sunday and have the team there to welcome you," he replied. "That's part of why I went in to the office on Saturday. It wasn't just to sign paperwork, but to get everything ready to hire you."

The crack deepened.

He set his glasses down on the table. "But then you saw the picture. You saw the updates. Everything that could go wrong, did."

"Why should I believe you?" I asked. In my heart, I wanted to believe him. I wanted to jump into his arms and forgive him everything if it were true, but he had hurt me too badly for me not to be at least a little careful.

He set his glasses down and focused the full power of his blue eyes directly on me. "Because I love you."

For a moment, I couldn't breathe. I couldn't speak, I couldn't move.

"I love you, Alicia," he continued. "I've loved you since that first day in the park. You're my perfect match. You're funny and smart, beautiful and creative. You see my work and know exactly how to make it shine. I would never do anything to hurt you. Ever."

"But how do I know?" I whispered. My heart felt like it was going to explode. The cracks in the armor around it were too deep to stop it from staying in one piece. "How do I know that you aren't just making this up. How can I trust you?"

He slid his phone across the stone table with the chess board printed on it. "Here's the credits for the game. If you want, you can call my update team and they'll tell you that I never took credit for the updates. It was always meant to be yours."

I cautiously picked up his phone and started reading. My name was featured prominently on the screen. According to the game data, it had been on there for the past two weeks. I'd been listed there before we'd had our fight.

"That's why you didn't want me to take the ZephTech job," I said quietly, sliding the phone back.

He nodded. "I almost asked you there at the restaurant, but I was so close to having everything be official that I wanted to wait. I see now that I shouldn't have."

I sighed. "Do you mean what you said before?" I asked, looking up into his eyes. "That you love me?"

"Yes. More than anything. I've missed you so much." His eyes said it was true. He was so genuine with his words. I wouldn't have been able to stay mad at him even if I had. Not now.

"I missed you, too," I whispered, choking back my emotion. "I love you, Jacob."

His smile was the sun. It made my world bright. "Can we try again? Please?" he asked.

I looked up at him. There was one more thing I had to tell him. "There's something you need to know. I meant to tell you before now, but..." I trailed off, not sure what to say.

"Nothing you say can push me away now," he said. I believed him.

"I'm pregnant," I blurted out. My eyes shot downward and I felt tears well in them. I didn't know what I would do if he reacted poorly.

He reached out his hands, folding them over my own. They were warm and strong and his very touch made my body react. I didn't want him to let me go. Ever.

"Look at me," he commanded.

My heart sank, and I didn't want to look up. Eventually, I lifted my eyes slowly. What I saw on his face melted my heart. He had tears welling up in his eyes as well.

"I couldn't be happier to add my first monster to my Monsterpedia."

I laughed. Naturally he'd find a way to turn this moment goofy. But that was why I loved him.

"And, hopefully, we'll add many more."

I nodded, unable to find the words that I wanted to say. There weren't really words to express the absolute joy in my heart.

"Maybe not one hundred and fifty, though. I'm not a Monster Go Master yet."

I finally laughed, tears flowing freely now. He leaned in and kissed me, right in the middle of the park for everyone to see. He kissed me like he meant it, like it was the first and last kiss of his life. He kissed me like I was the only thing worth living for and the only thing he'd ever wanted.

And I knew in that moment he was going to kiss me like that for the rest of my life.

EPILOGUE

"*A*re you sure?" Jacob frowned, holding up two nearly identical baby onesies.

"Yes, I'm sure. We only need one," I told him. "Babies grow fast. He'll be out of them before he's worn them twice."

"I don't know," Jacob said, shaking his head slowly. "We can't be too prepared."

I chuckled. "We already have fifteen of them at home. Maybe we could let my mom buy a couple of things for the baby, too?"

"I'm getting both," Jacob announced, putting both items in the basket.

I sighed. It was a good thing that Jacob was a billionaire. I was fairly sure that he'd already spent several million on this kid already.

A sharp pain started in my stomach and radiated around to my back. It wasn't awful, but it was enough to make me stop and gasp. Luckily, it didn't last long.

"Are you okay?" Jacob asked, coming to my side quickly. His blue eyes were big with concern. "Is it starting? Do we need to go to the hospital? I can leave all this stuff here, or I can have someone come buy it and meet us there or--"

"I'm fine," I interrupted him. "I think we're close. The doctor did say any day now, but I'm not going to pop this kid out right in the middle of the baby store."

"We should get you to the hospital anyway," Jacob informed me, taking my hand and abandoning his cart full of baby clothes and the size three diapers we apparently need right this minute.

I gently shook him off. "The contractions are still over ten minutes apart. I don't want to go to the hospital and get poked and pinched until we're actually sure they'll let us stay."

"They'll let us stay," Jacob assured me. "I made sure of that."

I rolled my eyes at him and laughed. Of course he did. He was more excited about meeting our baby boy than I could have imagined. It was all he talked about. Well, that and our business.

"Let's pay for our things and head home," I told him. "I'd like to shower in my own shower and get a couple more things put together. Then, when we're at the doctor recommended contraction level, we will head to the hospital."

Jacob frowned. "Are you sure?"

"Yes." I crossed my arms and glared at him.

He grabbed the cart and we quickly paid. Only one more contraction happened in the store, but I knew that it was starting.

We were going to have a baby in the next twenty-four hours.

I still couldn't believe it was happening.

The last eight months had flown by, yet they were the

happiest eight months of my life. They were also the busiest of my life, getting ready for this baby to come.

Then there was my new job.

He made sure I got full credit for all my update ideas and that I was settled in my new job at his company. I loved my job, and I loved the fact that I could do it from wherever I wanted.

Which happened to be our home. Jacob asked me to move in with him as soon as I told him about the baby. We decided that just moving in together wasn't enough. We wanted to be married when the baby came, so we had a simple ceremony with just our parents at the courthouse.

We had plans to do a full billionaire-style wedding once I had the baby and could pick out the dress of my dreams, but there was no hurry. I wasn't even sure that I really wanted a big wedding since the small one was so perfect.

Another contraction brought me back to the present. They were still far enough apart that I wasn't concerned yet. It was a process and I knew it wasn't going to be anything like the movies.

"Alicia," Jacob said, pulling the car to a stop. He turned and looked at me. "I love you. I just want you to know that. I love you so, so much."

I grinned and leaned over to kiss him. "I love you, too."

"I know that I've been a little nervous with the baby coming," he admitted. "But, it's just that I love you. That you chose me."

I grinned at him. "I choose you," I said. "Every day, I choose you."

THANK YOU!

*T*hank you for reading "I Choose You"! It was a bit of an experiment but I hope you really enjoyed it. If you did like it, consider leaving a review!

FAMILY DOCTOR'S BABY

amily Doctor's Baby

From New York Times bestselling author Krista Lakes, comes a sexy standalone novel about the baddest bad boy doctor and the sweet little nurse that he falls for.

When I left my small hometown years ago, I never expected to come back. I certainly never expected that when I did, I'd be working for *him*.

He's the town's doctor. He's supposed to be a respectable member of society, a pillar for the community. He's supposed to have come a long way from the bad boy who rode a motorcycle in high school.

But he hasn't. One glance from those lustful eyes looking at me tells me that he has the same voracious appetites that he did when we were younger.

Only it's not quite the same stare. It's more urgent. It's more intense. I'm not the same nerdy girl who tutored him.

I've grown up, developed fertile curves that I know he finds irresistible.

In this small town, rumors travel fast, and the family doctor can't be seen as a player. So he does try to resist. And I do too. But with every smoldering glance and moment of sexual tension, we find our barriers breaking down.

After a stressful night of touch-and-go baby delivery, a moment of elation overcomes our inhibitions. It seems like maybe we'll need to confront those rumors sooner rather than later, especially before I begin to show the results of that night.

Can I give this doctor the family he has always desired?

DR. MATTHEWS LEANED in and brought his lips toward mine. He paused right before our lips touched. Just for a moment, though. It was as if he were making sure that I wanted this. The universe held its breath as we both held our breath. I noticed everything from the way his aftershave lingered in the air to the water droplets in his hair. After a second that felt like eternity, he leaned in the rest of the way, firmly pressing his lips against mine.

Our fate was sealed.

A soft moan made its way up my throat as I relaxed into his kiss. I closed my eyes and let my hands drift up toward his face. His beard stubble tickled my fingertips as I dragged them over his cheeks.

It must have been the adrenaline we'd both experienced that morning. Or maybe it was that the emergency had bonded us closer than ever before. I didn't know what had gotten into either of us, but I suppose it didn't need explaining. It felt good and right and that's all I really cared about. I needed a release that only he could give me.

Jacob slowly broke our kiss and dropped his hands to the top of my hips. Then he leaned in again, passionately pressing his lips to mine. My heart began to do flip flops behind my rib cage. Within a few seconds, I felt Jacob open his mouth and gently dart his tongue out, teasing it into my mouth.

A tingling sensation coursed through my body as our tongues lightly wrestled with each others, twisting around in a sensual dance. I reveled in the sensations: his taste, his smell, the way he held his body against mine. This wasn't a dream. This was actually happening.

Jacob broke the kiss and took a step back. His cheeks were flushed and his eyes dark.

"I'm sorry. That was unprofessional."

My heart hammered in my chest and my lips ached for more of his kisses.

"I don't care," I told him. "I don't want to stop."

He looked up, his eyes bright as they met mine. Desire that matched my own shone in them and my body heated. I took the step forward to bring us back together. Slowly, I brought my hand up and wrapped it around the back of his neck.

"Are you sure you're okay with this?" he asked, his hands already coming to my hips.

"Just shut up and kiss me," I said, still smiling.

Family Doctor's Baby

ABOUT THE AUTHOR

New York Times and USA Today Bestseller Krista Lakes is a thirtysomething who recently rediscovered her passion for writing. She is living happily ever after with her Prince Charming. Her first kid just started preschool and she is happy to welcome her second child into her life, continuing her "Happily Ever After"!

Thank you for supporting an indie author. Anything you can do, whether it be writing a review, or even simply telling a fellow reader that you enjoyed this, helps me out immensely. Thanks!

Krista would love to hear from you! Please contact her at Krista.Lakes@gmail.com or friend her on Facebook!

Further reading:

Bad Boys and Babies
> Family Doctor's Baby
> The Billionaire's Baby Arrangement
> Crime Boss Baby

Kinds of Love
> A Forever Kind of Love
> A Wonderful Kind of Love

An Endless Kind of Love

Billionaires and Brides
Yours Completely: A Cinderella Love Story
Yours Truly: A Cinderella Love Story
Yours Royally: A Cinderella Love Story

The "Kisses" series
Saltwater Kisses: A Billionaire Love Story
Kisses From Jack: The Other Side of Saltwater Kisses
Rainwater Kisses: A Billionaire Love Story
Champagne Kisses: A Timeless Love Story
Freshwater Kisses: A Billionaire Love Story
Sandcastle Kisses: A Billionaire Love Story
Hurricane Kisses: A Billionaire Love Story
Barefoot Kisses: A Billionaire Love Story
Sunrise Kisses: A Billionaire Love Story
Waterfall Kisses: A Billionaire Love Story
Island Kisses: A Billionaire Love Story

Other Novels
I Choose You: A Secret Billionaire Romance
His Every Desire: A Billionaire Seduction
Wolf Six's Salvation: A Shifter Love Story
Burned: A New Adult Love Story
Walking on Sunshine: A Sweet Summer Romance
An American Cinderella: A Royal Love Story
Mr. Darcy's Kiss: A Contemporary Pride and Prejudice